MODEEN ROGUE

FRANK H JORDAN

The situations, organisations, and characters in this book are fictional, and any resemblance to an existing or past entity is entirely coincidental.

This book is written in Australian English.

Dedicated to all my loyal readers.
Thank you for sharing Jo's exciting adventures with me.

THE MISSION

- UNAUTHORISED AGENT ACTIVITY -

Decorated ex-Special Forces soldier and now national
security agent Jo Modeen struggles to come to terms
with the fate of close teammate Troy 'Wolf' Wolverton.
Critically injured during the team's most recent mission,
he lies comatose in Brisbane Hospital's intensive care
unit.
The prognosis for his full recovery?
Not good.
Driven to pursue the organisation responsible, Modeen
embarks on an unauthorised campaign of retribution. A
campaign that is both personal and perilous.
She's going rogue, and going alone.

CHAPTER ONE

In the dead of night, on the roof of a shopping complex in the main street of Noosa Heads north of Brisbane, a dark figure sat leaning against the one metre high parapet wall. The air was heavy with the threat of an approaching storm, and loud music thumped from the adjacent Shadows nightclub, located on the ground floor of the modern two-storeyed centre. Ignoring the throb of doof-doof music below, Jo Modeen kept her eyes fixed on the remote camera feeds streaming to the mobile phone in her hand.

There was movement in the left frame on the screen as a bronze, late-model Mercedes Benz nosed into the undercover carpark at the rear of the complex. Two men emerged from the sedan. One was beefy, dressed in an ill-fitting suit, with crude tattoos covering the exposed skin of his wrists, neck and face. The other man she knew by name.

Sergio Debeljah.

Tapping on his image to zoom in, she saw the Russian-born Australian tug down the jacket of his silver-grey pinstriped suit, gaudy rings glinting on his fingers and both wrists heavy with gold chains. When he raised a hand to brush a lock of greasy blonde hair off his face, Modeen gave a silent snort. His style of dress, classic boxer's nose, and penchant for flamboyant jewellery made Debeljah appear every bit the racketeering thug she knew him to be.

The two men disappeared from her screen as they entered the building. A short time later they reappeared in the right-side frame, their images projected there by the second remote camera focused at the window of the office above the nightclub. Swiping the frame left so that it filled the entire screen, Modeen scrutinised the room.

A good seven metres long by five wide, it had only one window to the outside. She watched the man with Debeljah stop at the gleaming, well-stocked private bar situated part-way down the left wall and begin pouring himself a drink. Debeljah continued sauntering toward the walnut, double pedestal desk at the right of the room, behind which sat a floor-to-ceiling bookshelf. A thick carpet, in a shade Modeen thought of as slime-green, added plushness to the already lavish space.

Glimpsing a figure in a far corner, she zoomed in on a man sitting tied to a chair with a black hood secured over his bent head. He was flanked by two more of

Debeljah's goons, one of whom elbowed the man in the head when he raised it as if to speak. Placing the mobile at her feet, Modeen rose to her knees and focused the parabolic reflector of her listening device on the top rear section of the building. Thumbing the volume control forward, she cupped a hand over the canal phone in her ear and heard Debeljah's guttural drawl.

'What does he know?'

'Not sure. We caught 'im stakin' out the lab,' the goon standing to the man's right replied. 'He was alone, boss.' Stepping forward, he handed Debeljah a small black wallet. 'Found this on 'im.'

Taking it, Debeljah seated himself behind the desk. He leaned back in the chair, opened the wallet and scanned its contents, and then closed it with a snap. 'Well, well. You've put us in a tight spot, Detective Sergeant Murphy.'

'It's only a tight spot if you make it one.' The muffled voice came from beneath the hood. 'You could let me go, and then we all walk away from this. I haven't seen any of your faces.'

'Hmm,' Debeljah drawled, 'it's a nice idea, but ... I don't think I'll do that.'

'Consider your next move carefully. You don't want to kill a cop!'

Laughter erupted in the room, then subsided abruptly as Debeljah raised a hand.

'I haven't seen anything.' Murphy's voice took on a

pleading note. 'And I have no idea where I am. Let me go and I swear our paths won't cross again.'

Debeljah caught the eye of the henchman leaning against the bar and lifted his chin. The man set down the half-full glass in his hand and hurried to the other side of the bar to mix a drink for his boss. Turning to the goon standing on Murphy's right, Debeljah gave a slow nod, at which the man took out a nine millimetre Beretta PX4 pistol from inside his suit jacket and began screwing on a silencer.

On the rooftop Modeen dropped the listening device at her feet. Pulling down a black balaclava to cover her face she straightened to her full height, yanked a Walther PPQ from her shoulder holster, and sprang on top of the parapet wall. While pulling back and releasing the weapon's slide she set off, leaping from the wall onto a section of curved corrugated iron awning. Sprinting toward the building's upper level, she raised the pistol and aimed at the side window.

Inside, the goon with the Beretta thumbed off the safety. About to press the silencer to Murphy's temple, he whipped his head around at the sound of fast-approaching feet outside the window. As a volley of bullets shattered the pane he gasped and cowered, as did all the room's occupants. And when shards of glass exploded inwards, Debeljah and his goons flinched and threw up their arms.

Modeen followed the fragments inside. Diving through the shattered window, she completed a smooth forward roll on the floor. Rising swiftly to one knee, she let loose two quick rounds from her silenced pistol, *blat blat!* The goons on either side of Murphy slumped to the ground beside his chair, lifeless.

She was turning her attention to Debeljah when the remaining henchman grabbed her from behind in a bear hug, knocking the gun from her hand as he did so. While struggling to free herself, she glimpsed Debeljah frantically rifling through a desk drawer, hunting for a weapon.

No time to waste.

She stomped hard on her attacker's leading leg, scraping the heel of her size nine combat boot down the front of his shin and digging it deep into his instep. He let out a howl and buckled forward. Feeling his grip loosen, she thrust her head back, cracking him under the chin.

His head flew back and he took a staggering step away, coughing and spitting broken teeth. When he screwed up his face and charged at her again, she took a wide stance, knees bent, preparing herself for the impact. The instant his heavy body collided with hers, she rolled her shoulders and used his momentum to launch him across the desk behind her. He slid over its polished surface, taking a laptop and lamp with him as he crashed into his boss, pinning him in the chair and against the bookshelf.

Debeljah had found his gun, but now his pistol arm was trapped beneath the dazed goon on his lap. Seeing him frantically shove the man aside to free his arm, Modeen dropped to the floor in front of the desk. Picking up her PPQ, she rolled onto her side and put a bullet in each of his knee caps. Debeljah gave a roar of pain and jerked back, his poised trigger finger contracting twice to fire stray rounds into the ceiling. All the violent movement was too much for the overloaded chair. It collapsed under their combined weight and he and the goon crashed to the floor.

The instant his head came into view, Modeen fired off another round.

Seeing Debeljah shudder and face-plant heavily into the carpet, a crimson stain seeping into the lush green pile around him, she sprang to her feet while the remaining goon scrabbled for the gun lying by his boss's limp hand. Leaning forward, she levelled her weapon at his temple. An instant later the books on the shelf behind him were sprayed a meaty red as his body slumped on top of Debeljah's.

And suddenly the thump of music from the nightclub was the only sound in the room.

Breathing hard, Modeen glanced over at Murphy, who'd clearly been straining against his bonds. The thick black wire ties securing his wrists had sliced into his swollen and in places lacerated flesh. His hood quivered as he whipped his head from side to side, trying desperately to comprehend what was happening around him.

She lifted the knife from the scabbard on her right calf and strode to his side. Feeling the eight inch blade slice through the ropes securing him to the chair, he flinched and sucked in a breath. Without speaking she pushed him off the chair and onto his knees, his wrists still bound behind his back.

'Who are you?' he blubbed. 'What's happening?' When the only response was another shove in the back which sent him forward onto his stomach, he sobbed, 'What's going on? Tell me!'

Modeen stood over him while taking a moment to survey the room. She stepped behind the desk to collect Debeljah's blood-spattered laptop from off the floor and the mobile phone from out of his jacket pocket, placing them on the ledge of the smashed window. Returning to Murphy, she knelt beside him and put a knee in the centre of his back. With a quick upward thrust of the blade, she cut his hands free while rising to her feet.

Finding himself released from his bonds he tried to stand, but she pushed him back down with one foot and held him there until he raised his hands as if in surrender. Once he was lying completely still she lifted her foot and then jogged to the window. Collecting the laptop and mobile, she sprang nimbly out and onto the roof, and was gone.

Murphy stayed frozen in place, uncertain whether or not to move.

Was this a trick? Was he being toyed with?

He strained his ears for any sound of movement. Hearing only the dull thump of the nightclub below, he gathered his nerve and slowly sat up, half expecting another shove in the back or punch in the head. When neither eventuated, he raised a tentative hand and pulled off the hood. Squinting in the sudden glare of the downlights, he blinked and anxiously scanned his surroundings.

He was the only person left alive in the room.

————

Lightning flashed brilliant white in her rear view mirrors as Modeen passed through Eumundi township, weaving her Kawasaki GTR through the sparse early morning traffic. Turning left onto the Bruce Highway she accelerated, taking care to stay just below the speed limit – attracting attention right now would be a bad thing – and set the big bike's cruise control. The trip home to the Gold Coast would take over two hours, and she was glad of the travelling time. It gave her a chance to wind down, for her adrenalin levels to return to somewhere close to normal.

The 1400 cc, shaft-drive GTR purred beneath her, slicing effortlessly through the heavy pre-storm humidity. When she hit a pocket of fresh, rain-cooled air, Modeen lifted her head above the bike's protective faring and raised her helmet's visor to let the wind rush against her face. It brought with it a sense of freedom, of cleansing, of carrying away her cares … briefly. She took a deep inhalation and lowered her head again. Dropping the visor back into place, she settled in to focus on the road ahead.

Back in her top floor apartment in Surfers Paradise she dropped her duffel in the corner of the master bedroom. Peeling off her black tee shirt and cargos, she headed to the ensuite bathroom for a long shower. While soaping her arms she discovered some remnants of the night's activities, a few tiny glass shards embedded in the skin. She carefully prised them out and then stood rolling her shoulders, letting the water wash over her face and down her back, loosening her taut muscles.

The digital clock beside her bed showed o-three thirty when she emerged wearing a white cotton singlet and matching shorts, and rubbing a thick towel over her short-cropped platinum-blonde hair. Catching sight of her duffel, she paused and then flicked the towel onto a chair. Finger-combing her damp hair she went to the bag, unzipped it, and stood gazing down at the mobile phone and computer she'd taken from Debeljah's office. She left them there, instead grabbing her own laptop off the dresser and climbing onto the bed.

While waiting for her laptop to boot up, she opened the bottom drawer of her bedside table and took out the memory stick she'd taped to the back of the drawer. Plugging the stick into the laptop's USB port, she opened a spreadsheet and clicked on a tab. When a list of names appeared on the screen, she scrolled down to the fifth entry, highlighting it and putting a line through the text.

Spruiking on social media wasn't smart, Debeljah, and neither was posting your private details. It made the job of finding you just too easy. You should've known better.

She saved and closed the spreadsheet and then the laptop, which she slid under the bed after removing the memory stick. Turning off the bedside lamp, she snuggled under the doona and was asleep within minutes.

CHAPTER TWO

It was o-nine hundred when Modeen surfaced. Yawning and throwing back the bedclothes, she stretched and then got up to shower and dress in jeans and a tee shirt. After making herself a quick breakfast she grabbed her leather jacket and was back on the GTR, riding north along the M1 freeway.

During the hour-long ride to Brisbane she allowed herself to think about Troy Wolverton and his surprise proposal before their last mission ... the mission that almost took him from her permanently, and left him lying unresponsive in the intensive care unit. Feeling her throat tighten and tears prick behind her eyes she made herself think of something else, and the second closest subject to her heart came to the fore.

Retribution.

She wanted those responsible for Troy's injuries to pay.

But even more than that, she wanted him back.

She stood in the doorway, gazing into the softly-lit private hospital room at the form lying on the bed. All was quiet, apart from the usual hums and beeps of the electronic monitoring devices in the room, and the background noise of a busy hospital ward. She took a deep breath and moved to the bedside, where she bent to press her lips against his lightly stubbled cheek. Perching on the edge of the bed, she gazed tenderly into his face. It was expressionless in repose, his eyelids shut and unmoving.

She closed her own eyes and pictured him smiling that crooked smile of his, thickly-lashed dark eyes crinkling at the corners, and felt her heart turn over as it always did. Swallowing the lump in her throat, she lowered her head to his broad chest and listened to the reassuring thump of his strong heartbeat. Hearing footsteps outside, she promptly sat up, expecting to see a nurse or orderly burst into the room. She was pleased when the footsteps continued down the corridor.

This was her private time with Troy. It was precious and she didn't want it disturbed.

Looking down at the hands resting by his sides, she took the nearest one in hers. It lay still in her grasp but was warm, and she could feel the latent strength beneath it.

Where there's life, there's hope. And I'm hoping you'll come back to me, Troy.

She ran her eyes over the equipment positioned around the bed and then fixed her gaze on him again. Very little had changed since her last visit. On the plus side he was still breathing on his own, and most of his superficial wounds had healed nicely or were barely visible. His left leg, while still in traction, had regained its normal colour. Gone were the purple bruising and inflammation. He remained lying motionless, however, partly covered by a crisp white sheet, and with the same assortment of wires and tubes connected to his body.

And yet….

Frowning, Modeen took a closer look. The tube up his nose that drained away gastric stomach contents and prevented aspiration into his lungs was still in place, as were the pads on his torso connected by wires to monitors recording his pulse and respiratory rate. The pulse oximeter that measured the amount of oxygen in his blood was still connected to the index finger of his left hand.

And then she realised what was missing.

The tube that had been attached to his skull to measure intra-cranial pressure was gone, replaced by a neat dressing. She frowned and brushed gentle fingers over that shaved area of his head. Squeezing her eyes closed and telling herself the removal of the tube was a good sign, she took a deep breath before opening her eyes again.

Saying brightly, 'Do you remember where we left off?' she reached into her carry bag and pulled out a paperback novel, Matthew Reilly's *Ice Station*. Opening it at the bookmark, she cleared her throat. 'I believe Scarecrow was about to use that maghook of his again.' She glanced at Wolf with a brave smile that didn't quite reach her eyes. 'I haven't heard of an Armalite MH-12, have you?' Painfully aware no response would be forthcoming, she carried on. 'I thought Armalite only made rifles. But that maghook is some versatile bit of gear, so if they're real, we should get one.' Lowering her eyes to the book, she launched into the story.

'Despite the searing pain in his side, Schofield....'

Aside from one quick trip to the coffee machine in the common room, she sat at Wolf's side reading aloud until her voice grew husky. Coming to the end of that chapter, she sighed, slipped the bookmark into the page, and slowly closed the paperback. She remained where she sat, holding his hand and staring into his face, until something told her they were no longer alone. Glancing toward the doorway, she saw a tall male figure silhouetted against the bright lights of the corridor. His face was in shadow, but she recognised him ... at least, she thought she did.

'Sorry, I wasn't staring. I just....'

That deep voice ... it made her heart leap, but she held herself in check.

He stepped into the room. 'You must be Jo. I was beginning to wonder if I'd *ever* meet you.'

There was a thread of tension in his voice, but she was too distracted by a rush of sensations to analyse it. She remained where she sat, staring silently at him. The way he moved, like his voice, was so familiar.

Achingly familiar.

But there was something about his stature ... it wasn't brawny enough. And then he spoke again, snapping her out of her stunned paralysis.

'Sorry, should've introduced myself. I'm Jake.' He gave a half-amused snort. 'Thought you might've seen the family resemblance....' When she continued staring mutely at him, he added tentatively, 'Troy's brother?'

Modeen blinked and nodded.

Jake Wolverton ... of course.

Rising to her feet, she put the book on the table beside the bed and then turned to shake Jake's outstretched hand. His grip was firm, though not as firm as his big brother's, she decided. They shared the same crooked smile, but there was a distinctive unease beneath the smile, and in his overall demeanour.

She said quietly, 'Nice to met you, Jake.' The hand-shake done with, she stood regarding him with a level, assessing gaze.

'You too.'

There was that unspoken tension again.

'I've been here for the past week.' His brow furrowed

and an accusing note crept into his voice. 'I expected to bump into you before this.'

So that's why he's so tense.

'I've been away on business the past four days.'

'Business?' One word, loaded with sarcasm.

'Yes.' She turned to look at Wolf. 'Apart from the removal of the tube in his skull, which I'm taking to be a good sign, there hasn't been any change in his condition.'

Jake exhaled. 'No.' He shook his head sadly. 'The doctors believe he could be comatose for months.' After a brief pause he burst out, 'Which is why I've arranged to have him transferred to Royal Hobart Hospital.'

Modeen turned to him with a frown. 'Transferred?'

'I'm taking him home. He needs to be close to family.'

'That's a bit sudden, isn't it?' She took a step closer and stared into his face. 'I've been visiting him every day, ever since he was injured. I only went away this week for—'

Jake raised a hand to cut her off. 'The decision's been made. I just got off the phone from his employer – and yours I guess – Mr Smith, who's been keeping me up to date on Troy's situation. He's agreed to organise the transfer, and has been most supportive and helpful throughout this … difficult time.' Jake fixed her with a steely-eyed look so reminiscent of Troy she had to turn away. 'You guys should count yourselves lucky to have such a good healthcare scheme attached to your jobs. Especially,' he added bitterly, 'in your line of work.'

She turned back to stare at him, an unspoken question in her eyes.

'Oh don't worry, Troy hasn't told me what it is you do for this NatSec mob. But I'm not an idiot, and I know my brother. There's no way a top-notch SASR sniper like him could stand being desk-bound in some safe little paper-pushing gig.' Pausing, he lowered his head, swallowed, and then continued more calmly. 'The doctors reckon if his condition doesn't improve and he stays like this for a prolonged time,' and he glanced over at the large, still form on the bed and then back at the floor, 'he may never come around. And even if he does, he may've suffered permanent brain damage … may even have lost the ability to walk and talk.'

He stopped speaking to drag a hand over his face. When he looked up at her, she saw his Adam's apple bobbing in his throat as he struggled to stay composed.

'They said to hope for the best but prepare for the worst, and the worst case for all of us, and especially for him, is that he awakens only to be bedridden or in a wheelchair for the rest of his life.' Jake's voice broke. 'If you know my brother as well as I think you do, you know what that would mean for him.'

Throwing him a curt nod, Modeen turned away to swipe an arm across her eyes.

For a man like Troy Wolverton to find himself in a situation like that was … unthinkable.

Unthinkable, and unbearable for those who loved him.

You can't let that happen, Troy … you've GOT to wake up, and as your old self.

As though in pain, she folded an arm across her stomach and bent her head. Swallowing the lump in her throat, she cradled her forehead in the palm of her free hand and tried to muster her courage, but all she could think was, *please wake up! Before you're taken away from me a second time.* She squeezed her eyes closed and warm tears spilled over to tumble down her cheeks. Swiping them away again, she ordered herself to get a grip and straightened to her full five foot eleven.

Reaching up a hand, she fingered the pendant on the chain around her neck. It lay where it always did, at the base of her throat, carefully tucked beneath the neckline of her shirt. She caressed it through the fabric, telling herself firmly, *as his next of kin, Jake has every right to have Troy transferred.*

She took a deep breath and, without turning to look at Jake, said brusquely, 'When is the transfer happening?'

'Tomorrow afternoon.' His voice was milder, as though he'd guessed how she was feeling. 'Look … I was going to discuss it with you but you weren't around, so I had to make the decision I felt was right for him.' He sighed and dragged a hand through his dark hair. 'I only agreed he could stay here for treatment initially because I knew he'd want to be close to you. But when I didn't see you all week….'

Her shoulders slumped and she gave a mute sideways nod.

'Of course you know you can visit him as often as you like in Hobart? That's what he'd want.' Receiving another silent nod in reply, Jake murmured, 'I'm flying back there tonight.'

Silence settled on the room again, broken only by the beep and hum of the machines. Rousing herself, Modeen moved to the bedside and tenderly brushed Wolf's fringe off his forehead. She bent to press her lips against his temple and then whispered in his ear, 'See you same time tomorrow. I love you.' Turning, she collected her bag from the visitor's chair and strode out of the room, giving Jake a tight-lipped nod as she passed.

She had just thrown her bag into one of the GTR's panniers when her mobile vibrated.

Damn! Forgot to take it off the silent setting.

She glanced at the caller ID and pressed Answer. 'Ben?'

'JD.' Ben's voice was clipped. 'I've been trying to contact you for the last two days. I've got news about Wolf.'

Looking down at the Messages app on her phone she saw a number of unanswered calls.

'Sorry, I've been ... busy.' Before he could speak again, she said, 'And I know about Wolf, I've just been to see him. The tube in his skull's been removed, and....' She swallowed hard to keep her voice from breaking.

'And his brother Jake is having him transferred to Hobart.'

There was a long pause and then Ben said quietly, 'I'm sorry, JD, there's nothing I can do about that. As Wolf's next of kin, it's Jake's call what happens to him.'

She exhaled and gazed down at her feet. 'I know.'

'His prognosis—'

'I know that too.' Her voice sounded strangled.

'He'll be with family there,' Ben said gently, 'so it might be for the best, JD.'

'Yes.'

'Now, why can I only reach you on your personal mobile?' Ben was all business again, and for that Modeen was grateful, it helped her get her emotions under control. 'Where's your NatSec phone?'

'Switched off.'

'Why?'

'I'm still considering my options. You did say I was on R-n-R, and could take a couple of weeks to think about my future?'

'You've got until Tuesday,' Ben answered crisply, 'when I want you here in Melbourne HQ for a team meeting with Spooky and Bugs.'

'I'll be there.'

'Right.' His tone was warmer when he continued. 'I hope you'll stay with NatSec, JD, but I'll respect your decision, whatever it may be.'

She exhaled and stared at the ground, murmuring, 'Thanks Ben. And I appreciate your patience.'

———

Modeen arrived at the hospital the same time the following day and headed straight to Wolf's room. She found herself holding her breath as she drew near his doorway, and only released it when she saw him still there. After giving him her usual hug and greeting, she took out the book and settled herself in the visitor's chair to read the next couple of chapters to him. When a passing nurse advised they would soon be prepping him for transfer, she nodded her thanks and closed the book.

Leaning her elbows on the edge of his bed, she took his nearest hand in hers. 'I'll leave the book with you, in case you wake up and—' Her voice caught in her throat and she bit her lip. 'Or we can carry on reading it together, when I come to visit you.' Pausing, she took a deep breath. 'They're moving you to Tassie, where you'll be close to Jake.' She swallowed, but the lump in her throat wouldn't move. 'I'll try and visit every chance I get.'

Taking a pen from her bag and opening the book, she wrote a message inside the back cover and then slipped the book into the top drawer beside his other personal items. Sitting back, she reached up to remove the gold chain from around her neck. A rose gold ring dangled from it, the diamonds embedded in the band glinting under the room's soft down-lights. Carefully lifting Wolf's head, she slipped the chain over it and then lowered his head to the pillow again.

'When you remember what this is and what it stands for,' she whispered in his ear, gently tapping the ring against his chest with a finger, 'you come and find me.' She brushed her lips over his and then wrapped her arms around him, resting her head on his chest. She stayed like that until her ears caught the sound of an approaching trolley.

Sitting up, she stroked the side of his face and murmured, 'I love you.' And when a nurse and two orderlies entered the room, she rose slowly to her feet.

'We need to prep him for transfer.' The nurse threw her a compassionate glance. 'I'm afraid you won't be able to see him again until he's settled in at Royal Hobart.'

Modeen nodded and took a final longing look at him before making her way out of the room. Keeping her head down, she strode along the corridor heading for the hospital carpark. Her NatSec Aurion waited there, packed with all her NatSec-issued equipment – mobile phone, computer, weaponry and assorted other gear – along with water and a few provisions, ready for the long drive ahead. Sliding behind the wheel, she entered the Melbourne address of NatSec HQ into the on-board GPS, which promptly informed her in a robotic voice that the trip would take nineteen hours.

She had three days to get there.

The GPS urged her to take the more direct inland route, but she tapped on some settings and finally convinced it to map the more scenic coastal route. Once on the Pacific Motorway, she would head south through Byron Bay, Coffs Harbour and Port Macquarie, and then overnight in Newcastle.

On checking the GPS for accommodation in Newcastle, she was presented with a lengthy list. Not wanting to waste time, she chose the Clarendon Hotel in Hunter Street. It had a rating of a little over four stars, was close to restaurants, and offered a low nightly tariff of only a hundred bucks.

That'll do.

She tapped on the link which connected her phone via Bluetooth, and proceeded to make the booking.

CHAPTER THREE

Modeen found the nine hour drive from Brisbane to Newcastle therapeutic. The powerful Aurion carried her in comfort, eating up the kilometres. And it felt good to be moving, to be *doing* something while pondering her next course of action.

At twenty hundred hours, the well-lit Clarendon Hotel appeared inviting and popular, judging by the number of cars parked nearby on both sides of the road. Modeen pulled into a loading zone across from the hotel and sat with the motor running while she surveyed the establishment.

The exterior of the two storey building was a tad stark and dated, but through the double glass doors at the front she saw a tastefully decorated lobby and a modern reception counter manned by smartly-dressed, smiling staff. Nosing out of the loading zone, she drove into the hotel's driveway and parked outside the front doors in a bay marked Short Term Guest Parking.

The check-in process was prompt and efficient, as she'd hoped it would be, and she soon found herself the occupant of a recently renovated, clean and comfortable suite. Heavy cream-coloured drapes had been pulled to the sides of the room's white casement windows, leaving a sheer curtain billowing in the gentle draft from the air-conditioner. An ornate oval mirror sat in pride of place on the burgundy-coloured feature wall. Below it the queen-sized bed sported crisp white linen and a tasteful chocolate-brown throw at its base, matching cushions and roll-pillow piled against the padded bed-head.

When she stood still and listened, and only the whisper of the air conditioner reached her ears, Modeen gave a satisfied nod. The door had closed behind her with a solid thud, and the room had an almost sound-proof feel about it, guaranteeing a peaceful night.

Yes, it would do just fine as an overnighter.

Dropping her duffel on the floor beside the bed, she glanced at her watch and decided to head downstairs for a meal before the restaurant closed. While she wasn't ravenous – her appetite had taken a hit after Troy was injured and was yet to resurface – the old Army saying *eat when you can, sleep when you die,* kept repeating in her head. She wasn't sure where the saying came from origi-nally – maybe an Aliens movie, or a Bon Jovi song? – but she recalled Troy barking it at a newly enlisted soldier who'd complained about the rations and lack of sleep during intensive training.

Back when their squad was stationed in East Timor … a whole other life ago.

Strolling through the hotel's up-market steak and seafood restaurant, which still bustled with patrons and harassed-looking wait staff, she opted for alfresco dining and made for the hotel's courtyard. The only other diners in the leafy, candle-lit area were a young man and woman, obviously in the throes of new romance. Their amorous murmurings and overt displays of affection had Modeen making for the furthest table from theirs. All the same, their voices carried and she found herself hurrying through her meal so she could make a quick exit.

With the man she loved beyond her reach, in every way that mattered, she didn't want to think romantic thoughts.

Back in her top floor room, she picked up her duffel and placed it on the bed. Taking out Debeljah's phone and laptop, she switched on the computer and sat on the bed to wait while it booted up. She pressed the phone's On button, and gave a contemptuous snort when it took her straight to the menu without prompting for a password.

Not big on security, were you, Debeljah? I guess you thought as the meanest kid on the block you didn't need to bother … wrong!

She scrolled through his contact list and checked the

names against the recent calls in the call log. Grabbing the hotel's complementary pen and notepad from the bedside table, she jotted down the names and numbers that caught her eye, in case they proved useful. Glancing at the laptop she saw it had booted up, also without asking for a password. She raised a scornful eyebrow and tapped the pen against her lips.

Careless, Debeljah, very careless.

Her search through the laptop's hard-drive revealed nothing out of the ordinary, and no new leads. The total lack of documents and spreadsheets stored on it was curious, though. When she checked his Internet browsing history, which was sleazy to say the least, she found nothing relevant to Debeljah's criminal activities. Clicking on a browser bookmark for his Yahoo email, she was confronted with a log-in screen.

OK ... so you were more careful about your messages.

Setting the laptop aside, she picked up his phone. She clicked on the email icon and a screen flashed up showing two unread messages.

This is just too easy!

A name in the email in-box caught her eye. Wiremu Kauri. It was a name she'd seen before. She opened the email and scanned its contents.

FROM: w.kauri@email.com.nz
TO: sergio.debeljah@email.com.au

Hi Serge.

Just wanting to confirm arrangements.

Meeting scheduled for 10am at my Dargaville office, 27th of next month.

Let me know what flight you'll be on and I'll have a car pick you up from Auckland airport.

Cheers,

Wiremu

Production Manager, Liquor Express

Dargaville 0310 New Zealand

After taking more notes, Modeen put down the pad and pen and was about to open another message in the in-box when she noticed the screen on the laptop beside her suddenly go black. Thinking it was just the screen-saver kicking in, or the computer conserving its battery power, she pressed the space-bar.

Nothing.

What the —?

She heard the hard-drive working and then a whirr as the computer's internal cooling fan cut in.

O-oh….

A hasty glance at Debeljah's mobile revealed the last fading pixels as its screen too went blank.

Someone's got smart and remotely wiped the laptop and phone operating systems.

Dumping the now useless phone on the bed, she sat back and stared at the ceiling.

They would've used remote tracking software to do that, which means – crap! – they know where I am.

Slamming the laptop shut, she leapt to her feet while checking her watch.

Almost midnight ... I've been working on the laptop and the phone for a couple of hours.

She slapped her forehead.

You idiot! Berating Debeljah for being stupid while all the time showing what a dumb-ass you are yourself!

Grabbing the note pad, she threw it into her duffel and then turned to Debeljah's phone and laptop. They were no good to her now, but she could throw them in one of the dumpsters in the basement carpark. That might keep the watchers guessing, for a short while at least.

She moved swiftly toward the suite's main door, only to stop in her tracks.

The basement....

That was where her car – and more importantly her weapons – were located. So near, and yet so far....

She blinked hard and exhaled through pursed lips before reaching for the doorknob. With ears and eyes peeled for any indication of movement, she cracked the door open and checked the corridor in both directions. Satisfied all was clear, she stepped out of the room. Taking care to close the door behind her with a soft click, she made her way soundlessly to the elevator, duffel slung over one shoulder and Debeljah's laptop held low by her side.

After punching the button for the lift she stood waiting, body poised, ears straining for any unexpected or unusual sounds and eyes alert for any peripheral movement. When a dull ping announced the elevator's arrival at her floor, she readied herself to enter it the instant the doors opened. But when they did, she jerked and stepped back.

Inside the lift, two islanders stood side by side, both dressed in dark suits and both pushing six foot. But while one was grossly overweight – so much so, it appeared his neck had subsided into his torso – the other was trim and athletically built. On seeing her, the boredom in their expressions vanished as their mouths fell open and their dark eyes widened to stare at her.

And then the big man moved. He flicked open his jacket, intending to reach for his gun, but Modeen had recovered first.

Dropping her duffel to the floor, she drew back her arm as if the laptop she was holding was a fourteen pound bowling ball she was about to launch down the lane. Instead of aiming at ten pins, she zeroed-in on the big guy and, with a powerful underarm thrust, slammed the computer's hard edge into his crotch. As he let out a gasp of pain and doubled over, bumping against the other man in the process and putting him off balance, she sprang forward and kneed the big guy in the face. His head snapped backward and slammed against the lift's rear wall.

With eyes rolling back in his head and looking like a

de-boned whale in a wrinkled suit, he slid down the wall, leaving a greasy trail on its mirrored surface, to land with a doughy thud on the floor of the lift.

Spinning anti-clockwise, Modeen used her momentum to crack the trim guy on the nose with a well-aimed elbow. Continuing the spin, she brought her other elbow around to follow through with a knock-out blow, but this time he was ready for her. Raising both forearms like a boxer he blocked the blow and pushed himself off the wall, forcing her to back out and into the corridor.

As the elevator doors began to close he stepped out to face her. His mouth twisted into a sneer, distorting the tribal tattoo that ran up the side of his neck and spilled onto his left jaw. He smoothed both hands over his spiked jet-black hair and took a wide, aggressive stance, staring at her with stone-cold eyes and looking every bit the Maori warrior.

She watched, whole body poised for action, as he reached up to unbutton his suit coat. Shrugging it off and revealing a snug-fitting, short-sleeved business shirt stretched over impressive biceps and pectorals, he flicked the jacket away and stuck out his chest. But Modeen's attention was focused on the jet black Glock nestled in the leather holster on his right shoulder.

He's armed and I'm not.

More old sayings ran through her head.

Pick your battles.

The best conflict is the one you avoid.

With that in mind, she thought about escaping down the stairs but with his body blocking the way, flight was not an option. She would have to stand and fight.

Surprised to see her opponent unexpectedly flash a grin, she eyed him warily as, with deliberate movements, he unfastened the buckle on the holster's breast strap and lowered it and the Glock to the floor.

Still leering at her, he took up a typical southpaw boxer's stance – right foot forward, arms up and fore-arms facing her, right fist leading. She eyed him coolly, taking his measure. Having sparred with plenty of ex-boxers in the Army, she recognised a left-hander and knew what to expect. It'd be *jab, jab* with the leading hand followed by left cross, right hook combinations.

And he didn't disappoint.

Rising to his toes he danced around her, inching forward, and then lashed out with the first right jab. She twisted away, at the same time snaking out a hand to grab his wrist. Pulling his arm forward and across her body, she punched him in the right ear. He gave a star-tled grunt and stumbled back, shaking his head.

While watching him dispassionately, she settled herself for the next attack. This time he looked more focused, less cocky. As he shaped up to her, she glimpsed the tattoo on his arm.

A black mamba snake.

Her eyes narrowed and the hairs on her neck stood on end.

Jab, jab, and then the left hook sailed past her cheek as

she faded right, having anticipated the move. Leaning in with her shoulder, she punched her fist into his other ear, her whole body weight behind the blow. This time as he staggered back she kept up the attack. A sharp kick to the groin followed by a driving stomp to his solar-plexus, bent him double and punched the wind from his lungs, sending him reeling into the wall.

Dazed and gasping for breath, he tried to straighten only to have his head snap sideways. Coming to a halt from the spinning back kick, Modeen watched his body slide down the wall and collapse in a limp heap on the floor. When he didn't move again, she bent to collect her duffel and his weapon. Removing the Glock from the holster, she pulled back and released the slide, and pressed the elevator call button.

The doors opened almost instantly, revealing the big guy still unconscious on the floor – obviously the lift hadn't been summoned since their first altercation.

Training the Glock on him, she entered the elevator and pressed the button for the basement carpark. She stepped over his prone mass to position her back against the lift's rear wall and kept the Glock trained on him. As the elevator came to a stop, he lifted his head a fraction and blinked as though about to come to. This earned him a crack on the temple from the heel of Modeen's boot, and a second face-plant into the grubby carpet.

She stayed to the side of the elevator as the doors opened, and took a quick check of the basement.

All quiet.

Stabbing a finger on the Door Open button to keep the lift stationary, she squatted beside the big guy and dug out his weapon and mobile phone. Rising, she took her finger off the button and then sent the lift to the top floor before stepping out. She made her way through the underground carpark, checking to right and left and she went. The Aurion sat where she'd left it. She unlocked the car and threw her duffel on the back seat, before slipping behind the wheel and putting the key in the ignition. A moment later she was speeding up the ramp and out into Hunter Street.

At that hour of the morning the city was reasonably quiet and the traffic scant, mostly taxis ferrying raucous young people to the next night club. Once satisfied she was far enough away from the hotel and wasn't being followed, Modeen pulled the car to the side of the road and picked up the big guy's mobile from the passenger seat. She switched it on and checked the recent calls log, cross-referencing the numbers with the list she'd made earlier from Debeljah's phone.

She paused, thoughtful, and then added a new number to her list.

Opening the driver's door, she leaned sideways and tossed the phone in front of the Aurion's rear wheel. Straightening, she closed the door again and tapped Resume Trip on the car's GPS. Too pumped to sleep, she figured she'd may as well start the ten hour drive and get there sooner rather than later. Besides, it would give her more time to think before the meeting with Ben.

As she accelerated away from the curb there was a satisfying crunch as the car's rear wheel crushed the phone into the tarmac. After a quick check in the rear view mirror, she settled back in her seat with a smirk.

Good luck tracking me now.

CHAPTER FOUR

Ten hours later Modeen arrived in inner city Melbourne. Negotiating her way through the thickening midday traffic, she rubbed her eyes. They felt dry and sore, and her eyelids, heavy. It had been a long drive from Newcastle, and a trip preceded by an unexpected altercation and hasty exit. She rolled down the Aurion's window to let cool, city-scented air rush into the warm cab. It felt good against her face, and she perked up a fraction. All the same, she was glad the meeting with Ben wasn't until the next day.

Not bothering with the GPS, she drove confidently in the direction of the Rydges Hotel. Like other interstate agents, she'd stayed at the Rydges before. It was an easy walk from NatSec HQ and offered clean, comfortable and quiet accommodations. Striding into its gleaming lobby a short time later, she felt a welcome sense of familiarity and security. The check-in procedure was prompt and efficient, and within minutes she was letting herself into a room on the tenth floor. Dropping the hotel key on the bedside table and her duffel on the floor nearby, she let herself fall, face-first and fully clothed, onto the bed.

And was asleep almost instantly.

Eighteen hundred hours glowed a soft green on the bedside clock. Modeen jolted upright at a second heavy rap on the door of her hotel room. Blinking her eyes into sharp focus, she sprang to her feet and then knelt to unzip her duffel and take out one of the Glocks she'd 'liberated' from the thugs in Newcastle. Dropping the clip into the palm of her hand, she felt its weight and nodded.

Full.

She palmed the clip into the base of the pistol, and pulled back and released the slide.

Narrowing her eyes when another loud thump came on the door, she rose to her full height and called, 'I'm coming.'

Crossing the compact lounge area to stand just inside the door, she held the Glock behind her back while turning the doorknob with her other hand.

'JD.' Ben Logan stood in the corridor outside, staring down at her from his six foot four muscular frame. He wasn't smiling.

'Ben, hey.' Taking care to keep the Glock out of sight,

she inclined her head and motioned him inside. 'Come on in.' As he went past, she tucked the pistol into the back waistband of her pants, tugging down her shirt to cover the bulge. 'How'd you know I was here?'

He didn't answer straight away. Striding across the room, he stood at the window as though taking in the view. In the gathering dusk, lights were blinking on all around the city.

Without turning he replied, 'Leanne.'

At the mention of NatSec's resource manager, Modeen gave a slow nod. Leanne Martin oversaw agents' needs, travel arrangements and other resources, some of which were not available by any other means.

I'm going to miss that support.

'I asked her to let me know when you'd checked in,' Ben went on. 'She also advised that you didn't *fly* here from the Gold Coast.' He flicked Modeen a sideways glance. 'We can still track your NatSec phone and vehicle even when we can't track you.' Lifting his chin, he indicated the tiny scar on her arm where she'd removed her personal tracker. That piece of clever tech had enjoyed a brief stint in her aunt Hannah's handbag, but was now safely back in Modeen's duffel.

Ben turned to the window again. 'Am I right in thinking you plan to hand in the car, along with your notice?'

When she didn't answer, he lowered his head and clamped both hands on the edge of the broad window sill. When he spoke again it was with a note of resignation in his deep voice. 'I thought so.' He sighed and then turned to face her. 'Look, I wanted to talk to you before the meeting tomorrow ... unofficially.'

'I see.' Modeen lowered herself to perch on the edge of the sofa diagonally opposite him.

He sat too, on the window ledge, with his long legs stretched out in front of him. After gazing at her for a long moment, he said quietly, 'I had hoped you'd take advantage of our employee counselling service.'

She looked down at her hands. 'I appreciate your concern, Ben, but I'm fine. I don't need counselling.'

He sat forward, resting both elbows on his knees and clasping his hands together between them. 'The situation with Wolf has gotta be tough on you, especially now he's been transferred to Hobart.' Receiving a tight-lipped nod in reply, he continued more gently. 'Wolf's tough, so don't give up on him, JD.' He gave a humourless grunt. 'If anyone can come through this, it's Troy Wolverton.'

'I'd never give up on him,' she said brusquely, 'nor will I *ever* stop hoping he'll come out of this alright.' Raising her head, she fixed her eyes on his. 'After the meeting tomorrow with you and the guys, I'm flying to Hobart.'

He nodded and held her gaze. After a long pause, he said, 'I know you're aware of all this, but I need to make sure you've thought things through, that you're not acting on impulse.' When she opened her mouth to speak, he held up a hand to silence her. 'If you resign from NatSec, you'll lose all access to the resources the organisation can provide. The protection afforded you as one of our agents will be withdrawn, you'll be on your own. If you run into trouble the team and I won't be able to help you, much as we'll want to.' Exhaling deeply, he lowered his gaze to the floor.

'I understand.' Her lips barely moved as she murmured the words.

He raised his head to stare at her, his dark eyes flinty. 'And if you continue to pursue members of the cartel responsible for what happened to Wolf, your actions won't be sanctioned. You'll be working outside the law. If you're caught, you could be convicted of assault, manslaughter, or even murder. How will it help Wolf if you end up locked away for life?'

She stared at him for a long moment before muttering through tight lips, 'What makes you think I've been pursuing the cartel?'

He raised a disbelieving eyebrow. 'Let's not play games, JD. I recognised your work in Bunbury when one John Reger of the Black Mambas took a fall – literally. And having been advised that the bodies found at the scene were those of Black Mamba member Sergio Debeljah and his associates, I suspect the events in Noosa two days ago were also of your doing.'

When she didn't confirm or deny his allegations, Ben sighed. 'On the plus side, I know of one extremely grateful detective sergeant who'd very much like to thank the person responsible for saving his bacon.'

'What was the DS doing there, by the way?'

'He was on a stake-out, and got careless.'

A smile flickered across her face and then was gone. Locking eyes with him again, she said stiffly, 'I want out, Ben,' and then corrected herself. 'Make that *need*. I *need* to get out.' She paused. 'And this isn't the Army, I can leave whenever I choose … isn't that right?' At his frowning nod, she exhaled and dragged fingers through her hair, murmuring, 'Things were different when we were in the military. For one thing, I wasn't *involved* with anyone in our unit.' Shaking her head, she gazed down at her hands. 'I guess it was foolish of me and Wolf to start a relationship. In our line of work, an attachment like that is a distraction to say the least. And now we're paying the price for our foolishness.' Lifting her chin, she said stoutly, 'But I love him, and nothing will *ever* change that.'

'Then go to him. Forget about the Black Mambas. They were dealt a hefty blow when we shut down their drug operation, and again when you took out Reger. He was the one directly responsible for Wolf's injuries and now he's out of the picture. Surely that's reason enough to let it go. Please, JD, for everyone's sake.'

She could feel his appeal undermining her resolve. Springing to her feet, she walked to the small dining table and bent to rest both hands on its laminate surface. Keeping her back to Ben, she stared unseeingly down at the table top and said in a strangled voice, 'The Black Mamba organisation is bigger than Reger and Julia Creek.'

'Yes it is.'

'So … is NatSec planning to actively pursue them?'

Ben winced at the thread of hope in her voice. Seeing her shoulders slump at his muttered, 'Not at present,' he hastened to add, 'but the instant they're once more deemed a threat to national security, you can rest assured they *will* be pursued.'

She whispered bitterly, 'Not deemed a threat …,' and thumped the table with a fist. 'Wolf is in a coma because of them *and* because of me, Ben. He should've stayed at his post. From there he could've taken out that chopper easily. But instead he came running to h-help me and—' Her words caught in her throat and she choked back a sob.

'You can't put all that on yourself, JD.' Frowning, Ben pushed off the window sill. 'We don't know for sure why Wolf left his post, it may've had nothing to do with you at all.'

Recalling Troy's words to her just before their last mission, she squeezed her eyes closed as her misgivings at the time returned to taunt her.

… I've never had the slightest cause to worry about his focus on the job before this …

Sucking in a shuddering breath, she blinked away tears. 'I wish that were true, Ben, I really do. But I know it had *everything* to do with me.' She went to clutch at the chain around her neck, only to have her searching fingers come up empty. And then she remembered. She'd given it – *returned* it – to him. She let her hand drop to her side and swallowed again, feeling Ben's eyes boring into her back.

'Why do I get the feeling I've been wasting my breath?' He shook his head. 'Look, I picked you all those years ago to join my SASR unit, despite opposition from a number of quarters, because I knew you had a good moral compass and wouldn't let the team down under any circumstances. Are you sure your compass wasn't knocked out of whack by what happened to Wolf?' He gave a resigned sigh. 'I know what that feels like … after all, I chased the SoA all the way to Afghanistan to ensure my family was safe. But I stayed with NatSec the whole time. If you're so hell-bent on getting even with the Mambas for what they did to Wolf, why don't you do the same? That way, when they pop up on our radar again – and they will – you'll have your chance at retribution with all the support and resources of NatSec at your disposal.'

Taking a deep breath, she snapped, 'Once I've resigned, what I do is my business. It affects me and no one else. And right now, that's the way it has to be. I don't want to feel responsible for another team member's injuries, or even be around when it happens. And we both know it can happen at any time, to any one of us.' Her voice wavered. 'Case in point, Troy.'

'JD—'

'End of discussion, Ben.' Turning, she marched into the bedroom and moments later was back, standing in front of him holding out an envelope. 'You may as well take this now.' She pressed her lips together before saying tightly, 'I'll say my goodbyes to you all at tomorrow's meeting.'

Slowly reaching out a large hand, he took the envelope from her and, without opening it, slipped it into the inside pocket of his suit jacket. 'Can I at least shout you one last dinner, tonight?'

She smiled sadly. 'Thanks, but I'd be lousy company, Ben. Go home and be with the most important people in your life. Emily and Chelsea will be waiting for you.'

'And it's thanks to you that they are.' He gave a resigned exhalation. 'Very well, JD. I'll see you at o-nine hundred.'

Closing the door behind him, Modeen pressed her back against it and shut her eyes. She stayed that way, calming herself by listening to her own breathing, before heading to the bedroom to return the Glock, now warm from her body heat, to her duffel. Emerging from the bedroom, she went into the kitchenette and made herself a coffee. With steaming mug in hand she went to the sofa, flopped onto its padded comfort, and rested her feet on the coffee table. She was just draining her cup when another knock came on the door.

About to make for the bedroom and her duffel again, she stopped in her tracks when a gruff voice from outside called, 'Yo, Modeen, suit up! We're headin' out for some grub.' There was no mistaking Barry Pritchard's larrikin voice. Smiling, she strode to the door and opened it. Her smile widened when she saw not only

Barry, AKA Bugs, standing there but also Luke Jackson, AKA Spooky.

'Hey guys.'

At her warm greeting, and without waiting to be invited, they trooped inside, fist-bumping her as they passed. Checking the corridor was clear, she closed the door again saying pensively, 'Did Ben send you?'

Bugs frowned. 'We ran into him downstairs on his way out, but *send* us? Why would he do that?' When she didn't answer, he gave his trademark toothy grin and flopped onto the sofa, resting his hands behind his strawberry blonde head. 'We're just here for the meeting tomorrow, same as you, and thought we should grab the chance to catch up over some chow.'

Spooky remained standing, eyeing her sceptically. 'Why would you think Ben sent us? What's going on?'

Modeen sighed. 'He was just here, and ... well, you may as well know ... I've handed in my resignation.'

Both men stared back at her wordlessly. Finally Bugs said, 'Yeah ... we wondered if that might've been on the cards. You wanna be by the wolfman's side, right?'

'We heard he's been transferred to Hobart,' Spooky cut in. 'Has his condition changed?'

Modeen swallowed and tried to sound positive. 'The tube's been removed from his skull, which I guess is an improvement. But he's still unresponsive.'

Nobody spoke for a while, and then Bugs leapt to his feet. 'No guess about it, that's a definite improvement! So let's go chow down and celebrate it.'

'I warn you, I'm not good company at the moment.'

Striding over to grasp both her arms, Bugs stared down at her and said solemnly, 'Y'know, Wolf wouldn't want us to sit around mopin'.' As he spoke, his tummy gave a loud rumble, and without losing stride he added just as solemnly, 'And with our stomachs growlin'.'

She shook her head in reluctant amusement and murmured, 'I know.'

'So it's settled then.'

Seeing her shrug of capitulation, Spooky clapped his hands together. 'Good. So what do we feel like eating tonight? Italian, Thai, Greek? It's all on tap in Lygon Street.'

Modeen smiled. 'You guys decide while I take a quick shower.'

'Glad you said that.' A grinning Bugs pointed at her crumpled, slept-in clothes and tousled hair and threw Spooky a wink. 'I didn't wanna have to start droppin' hints. My ex reckons I suck at tact.'

In the end they chose Italian, and considering Lygon Street was known locally as 'the Italian Precinct', it wasn't hard to find a cosy little restaurant sporting red and white checked tablecloths, and emitting lip-smacking aromas of warm garlic and parmesan cheese. The deal was clinched by the chubby, balding man standing by the doorway, wiping his sweating face on the apron tied around his bulging midsection. He beamed at everyone who passed and waved a wine bottle in the air, booming in a thick Italian accent, 'You dine-a my place, I give-a you red wine, on-a the house!' When he spotted Modeen, his eyes widened and he called, 'Bella signora! For you, I give-a *two* bottles.'

After showing them to a table near the rear of the restaurant, the fat man made good on his promise by presenting them with chilled bottles of 'real Italian' lambrusco and promptly filling their glasses. Once happy they were settled and perusing the menus, he clapped his hands and wished them a pleasant meal, before taking up position outside once more.

As soon as he was gone, Spooky turned to Modeen. 'I've got a bone to pick with you.'

'Oh?' Taken aback, she frowned at him.

'Yeah,' Bugs chipped in. 'Me too.'

'Why? What have I done ... or not done?'

Leaning closer, Spooky said quietly, 'What's the big idea going after Reger by yourself? Ben sent me and Bugs after him. You were supposed to be out of the picture.'

'Oh ... right.' She looked chagrined. 'Well, you see, I got hold of some intel that needed to be acted on fast, but you two were on your way to Sydney. Which reminds me, did you find anything interesting down there?'

'Nah.' Bugs shook his head and drained his wine glass. 'Just some more seedy nightclubs, owned by Rotorua Holdings. We were tryin' to get a lead on Reger.'

'Rotorua Holdings ...,' Modeen mused aloud. 'I'd

forgotten about them.' She gave a slow nod. 'They paid for the hire cars used in the Olman hit.'

'Yeah.' Spooky took up the story while Bugs re-filled his glass. 'But we drew a blank. Ben was monitoring all flights departing Australia at the time, and suggested we check out a place of interest in Perth before heading to New Zealand. But when you got to Reger first, we were recalled.' He paused to give her arm a gentle fist bump. 'We're going to miss you, Modeen. That radar of yours has gotten us out of some potentially nasty situations.'

Bugs nodded. 'You bet we're gonna miss ya.' Raising his glass, he announced with somewhat less than the usual gusto, 'Who dares wins.'

Turning the Aurion into a one-way lane between two towering buildings the following morning, Modeen nosed the car to a stop in front of the solid boom gate spanning the lane's narrow width. Buzzing down the window, she waved her entry card at the sensor mounted on a pole to the right of the gate. There was an audible click and then the boom rose.

She continued down the solid concrete ramp only to stop again at an imposing steel roller door, where she stuck her head out of the window to stare at a camera mounted on the wall. Nothing happened for a few seconds, and then she heard a loud clunk followed by a metallic groan as the door began to rise. While waiting for the door to finish its upward climb, she glanced at her watch – ten minutes to nine, right on time for the meeting with Ben. The door came to a stop and with a fleeting squeal of fat tyres on concrete, she guided the Aurion into the subterranean carpark.

Her footsteps rang in the carpark's hollow silence as she strode to the elevator, a large envelope in hand, and swiped her card to summon the lift. It arrived with a swish of doors and she stepped inside. There were only two arrows on the control panel, one up and one down. The down arrow blinked while the up arrow was greyed-out, indicating the lift would go no higher. She pressed the down arrow and felt the elevator carry her one level below.

A second later the doors opened onto a familiar corridor. To the left it ended abruptly in an imposing door fitted with a gleaming metal keypad, and to the right a guard was stationed at a counter behind a bulletproof glass security panel. The counter extended past the panel, with a revolving door and small conveyor on one side of it and a podium fitted with a built-in digital touch screen and speaker on the other.

The guard's expression didn't alter at her approach. Eyeing her levelly he said, 'Please identify yourself, Ms Bennet.'

'G'day Stan.' Her eyebrow twitched. 'Look, you know who I am, so why go through all this rigmarole?'

'Please identify yourself, Ms Bennet.'

She rolled her eyes and exhaled, thinking, *if this bloke ever tried to smile his face would crack.*

The conveyor hummed into motion and the blank screen on the podium blinked to life, displaying the outline of a hand. Placing the envelope on the conveyor, she watched it disappear through a curtain of rubber strips to pass beneath a security scanner. Then she stepped up to the podium, put her hand directly onto the screen, and in a clear voice said, 'Josephine Bennet.' The outline turned green and flashed as thread-like yellow shock waves radiated from each finger tip.

From out of the speaker a robotic voice announced, 'ID confirmed,' as the words *Agent Josephine Bennet* flashed on the screen above her hand.

Tilting his head toward the revolving door, the guard said in the same monotone, 'You may proceed.' He flicked a toggle switch on the control panel beneath the counter and the door whooshed into motion. At the same time the conveyor slowed and came to a halt.

Modeen stepped through the door and collected her envelope from the other side of the scanner, before making her way along another narrow corridor to a set of elevator doors. The control panel on this lift offered a choice of three lower levels. She punched the button for one floor down. When the doors opened, she stepped into an expansive open plan office area positioned around a leafy central atrium. Water tumbled from a fountain in its centre, creating a soothing backdrop.

Skirting the administration work stations positioned around the atrium, nodding greetings to staff members as she passed, she headed for the offices at the far end of the room housing the team leaders and operations manager. When she knocked on Ben's office door, she was met by a grinning Bugs and a waft of second-hand garlic.

'Hey, Modeen.' He thumped her on the shoulder with a large, friendly hand. 'Come on in, we just got here ourselves. And don't worry, I've already apologised for our garlic breath.' He turned to Ben with a shrug of broad shoulders. 'That's just the price you pay for eatin' Italian tucker.'

'The price everyone *else* pays, you mean,' Ben muttered gruffly as he rose from behind the desk. He nodded. 'JD,' and indicated a vacant chair. 'Have a seat.'

Spooky too rose to greet her with a smiling, 'Modeen.'

'I'm glad you could all make it,' Ben said. 'I wanted to take advantage of this rare opportunity for the team to get together.' He waited until everyone was settled before resuming his own seat. 'Spooky will be heading back to Fremantle tomorrow, and Bugs....' He paused to take a breath. '... will be taking over Wolf's station in Canberra, for the interim.'

Clasping her hands in her lap, Modeen bent her head and nodded as Ben went on.

'Bugs and Spook are aware of your decision to leave NatSec, JD.' He frowned. 'And I believe they feel the same way about it as I do.'

At their murmurs of agreement, he continued. 'I want to make it clear that your resignation is accepted with regret. But I understand it's your decision, and yours alone.' He gave a resigned exhalation. 'I've arranged for you to have a debrief with James. As I'm sure you know there's an agent exit process, paperwork for you to sign, etc, after which I'd like you to report back here.' His lips tipped upward but his eyes and tone remained sombre. 'Then I'll take you all out for lunch.'

Rising, Modeen dropped the keys to her NatSec Aurion on top of the A4 envelope and slid it across the desk to Ben. 'Everything's in there, all my NatSec passports, swipe cards and documentation.' Without meeting his eyes she said, 'And thanks for the offer, but I'll have to skip lunch. My flight leaves for Hobart at thirteen hundred.'

Ben nodded. 'Of course, you want to be with Wolf.'

'Yes.' Pausing to glance at her two team mates, she said in a tight voice, 'Besides, we said our goodbyes last night.'

She made to move away and then stopped. 'Oh, yeah.' Pushing her index finger and thumb into the tiny coin pocket in the front of her jeans, she tugged out a small metal object. 'This is NatSec's too.' Leaning forward, she put it on the desk beside the envelope and keys.

Ben picked up the agent tracking device and turned it over in his fingers. Rising to his feet, he moved to stand in front of the desk. 'Well then, I guess this is goodbye.' He was about to extend a hand to shake hers, but instead pulled her in for a hug, saying gruffly, 'I'm not in the habit of hugging agents, but … we're going to miss you, JD.'

Spooky and Bugs rose to do the same and then Bugs opened the door for her. 'See you 'round, Modeen.'

Biting her lip, she made to leave only to stop in the doorway when Ben called, 'JD.'

She glanced back to see him lob something at her with an underarm throw. 'I'd like you to keep this.'

She caught it in her left hand and looked down at her palm. It was her tracking device.

When she raised questioning eyes at him, Ben said, 'For my peace of mind.'

With a slow nod, she slipped it back into her coin pocket and left.

The three men took their seats again, looking thoughtful. Frowning after her and shaking his head, Ben murmured, 'I'm worried about her.'

'Any particular reason?'

Ben flicked Spooky an anxious glance. 'If Wolf doesn't pull through….' He didn't need to elaborate, the other two knew what he was thinking.

Spooky sat forward. 'She's strong Ben, she'll cope with whatever happens.' He frowned. 'I know Wolf is special to her, but it's not like she hasn't been down this road before. We've all lost close friends in the service.'

Ben said sharply, 'This is about retribution.'

'But Foster's dead and she's taken Reger out of the picture,' Bugs cut in. 'There's no one left to pursue, she's had her retribution.'

Sitting back in his chair, Ben said quietly, 'I don't believe she'll stop until *everyone* associated with Reger or the Black Mamba organisation is made accountable.' When the others gaped at him, he sat forward again and drummed his fingers on the desk. 'It's just a feeling.' Clearing his throat, he said briskly, 'Now Bugs, you on track with the move to Canberra?'

———

The flight from Tullamarine had her disembarking an hour later at Hobart's international airport, located seventeen kilometres north-east of the city in Cambridge. From the arrivals hall Modeen made straight for the hire car booths, and shortly after headed outside to claim her Hyundai Getz. Calling up the map app on her mobile, she keyed in Royal Hobart Hospital and then studied the screen briefly before nosing the compact hatch into the traffic.

The harried receptionist manning the hospital's main desk directed her to room seventeen in H Block on the third floor. As she neared the room, Modeen heard a commotion coming from inside and quickened her pace.

'No, No, NO!' an irate female voice exclaimed. 'You can't bring that *creature* in here! This is a *hospital.*'

'But Sebastian is no trouble,' another female voice wheedled.

'It doesn't matter. This is a clean zone and dogs are unhygienic.'

'But pets are supposed to be good therapy for patients.'

'I don't *care*, take that thing outside the hospital *now!* Or I'll call the orderly and have you *both* removed.'

Modeen arrived in the doorway to see Jake Wolverton standing on the far side of Wolf's bed, face buried in his hands and shaking his head. A red-faced woman – Jake's wife, Modeen assumed – stood on the near side of the bed, a large handbag slung over her shoulder with the little head of a Shih Tzu protruding from the top of it. A middle-aged woman in white, obviously a Registered Nurse, stood nearby, her whole body stiff with disapproval.

With a stomp of her foot, 'Dog lady' huffed, 'Come on, Jake, we know when we're not wanted.'

At the churlish words the scowling RN's expression only grew more determined. Crossing her arms over her chest, she tapped the toe of her shoe as though on a count-down.

With another loud huff, Jake's wife stomped past the nurse and out of the room without even glancing at Modeen. Wearing an appropriately hang-dog look Jake went to follow his wife, but on seeing Modeen in the doorway his face brightened and he was about to speak when an imperious voice called from the corridor, 'Come *on*, Jake!' Frowning, he gave Modeen an apologetic shrug and muttered, 'Sorry,' as he hurried past.

Modeen watched them go and then turned her attention to Troy, who lay motionless amidst all the commotion.

With hands on hips, the RN turned interrogative eyes on her and barked, 'Are you family?'

'No, just a close friend.'

'Well, thank Heavens for small mercies.' With a loud exhalation and a roll of eyes, the nurse turned on her heel and marched from the room.

Now alone with him, Modeen approached the bed, saying softly, 'Hey Troy. I'm back.' She ran her eyes over the monitoring equipment around the bed and then bent to stare into his closed face for a long moment. Dropping a kiss on his forehead, she took his nearest hand in hers and perched beside him. Recalling his account of his last visit with his brother and sister-in-law, she said brightly, 'So I guess that was Jake's Amber and the little shit … er … Shih Tzu?' Chuckling to herself, she ran a caressing hand down the side of his face, feeling the rasp of five o'clock shadow on his jawline.

Whispering, 'I know you're in there somewhere,' she bit back tears and glanced at the bedside table. Seeing the book she'd been reading to him in Brisbane sitting there, she grabbed it and leafed through to the marker near the middle page.

'Do you remember where we left off?' She flicked back and forward a few pages from the marker. 'Hmm … I might need to refresh my memory. Hope you don't mind if I start a few pages back.'

After settling herself more comfortably, she stayed there reading aloud for the next few hours.

Coming to the end of a chapter she closed the book and put it back on the table. Gazing into Troy's immobile face, she murmured, 'I'll be staying in Hobart for the rest of the week,' before planting another kiss on his forehead. 'So I'll see you tomorrow.' With a final squeeze of his hand, she rose and left, pausing to take a final look back at him from the doorway.

On her way out she stopped at the ward sister's desk, where the aggro RN sat with a bunch of patient charts in front of her. When she looked up, Modeen asked quietly, 'How is he doing?'

The RN regarded her assessingly before answering, 'He's only been here a couple of days, but his condition is fairly stable.'

'So no change, no improvement?'

'Not in his overall condition, but now his leg has healed sufficiently, his physiotherapist can increase the exercise component of his treatment. His muscles are already responding to it.'

Modeen frowned. 'Exercise?'

'Yes, it's a new therapy proving beneficial in cases like Troy's. Prolonged bed rest results in muscle atrophy, which causes significant delays in post-coma recovery. Exercising the biggest muscle group in the body helps reduce overall loss of muscle tone.'

'But how?'

'His feet are strapped to a cycle machine for an hour or so while he's lying in bed.'

Mixed emotions crossed Modeen's face. While glad he was receiving the best and latest treatment, the thought of Troy's body being manipulated without his knowledge felt wrong. But then....

'This will help speed his recovery when he comes out of the coma.' Seeing Modeen's expression, the RN added, 'The neurologist also says having visitors spend time with patients like Troy, talking to them like everything's normal, is good therapy. So keep it up, love.'

Modeen took those words to heart, spending most of the next day and the one after it at Troy's bedside. She read to him, held his hand, chatted to him about everything and nothing, all without any glimpse of response. By the end of the week, she was on first name terms with the RN and other ward staff, and had run into Jake – minus Amber and the Shih Tzu – a few times.

While still reserved around her, Jake appeared pleased she was visiting his brother. He readily shared the ward doctor's comments about how well Troy's physical injuries were healing, and the physiotherapist's satisfaction with his response to the in-bed exercises. He also passed on a warning from the neurologist.

'Should—' he began, and then winced. 'I mean *when* ... he recovers consciousness, we've gotta let Troy regain his memories in his own time. The neurologist stressed that it would be detrimental to his recovery to feed him his memories, or to expect him to remember everything in the first instant. But that's gonna be hard. Troy's not one for takin' things slowly.' Jake's face worked as he struggled to keep his emotions from showing.

So like his brother.

With her heart in her throat, Modeen could only nod.

Sitting beside Troy's prone body the next day, she cradled his warm hand in both hers. 'This is my last visit for a while, Troy. I'm going home to the Gold Coast for a few days. But I'll be back as soon as I can.' She bent to press her lips against his brow and stayed that way for a long moment, breathing in the warm male scent beneath the smell of antiseptic soap on his skin. Slowly rising, she tucked his hand by his side and then got to her feet. Her footsteps were heavy, reluctant, as she walked to the doorway.

When she turned for a final look at him, lying still and silent and alone, her eyes stung and her throat tightened. Blinking hard, she turned and strode away.

CHAPTER SIX

Phillips Lane in the outer Sydney restaurant precinct was cold, dark, and reeked of stale booze and urine. Foul-smelling dumpsters lined the left side of the lane, convenient to the rear entrances of several restaurants and a noisy nightclub. And at that time of night things were hotting up in the club.

Its back door banged open and a gaudy glow from multi-coloured lights and a rotating disco ball spilled into the lane way, accompanied by the thump of music and shrill babble of voices. A partly dressed young couple, pawing at each other, almost fell out of the door onto the bitumen. Unlocking lips long enough to giggle drunkenly, they staggered down the lane and away. From within the shadows the bag lady watched them go before once more turning her attention to the contents of the closest dumpster.

Every now and then the back door of a nearby restaurant opened, releasing wafts of lip-smacking aromas along with the clatter of pots and pans and hollered instructions from chefs, as harassed-looking kitchen hands charged out to the lane carrying bags of scraps. Taking care not to get too close to the roach and rodent-ridden dumpsters, they hurled their cargo with practised skill into the bins and then scurried back inside, wiping their hands on their aprons as they went.

The bag lady ignored all the bustle and kept low in the dumpster she'd commandeered, rummaging through the rubbish with her filthy mittened hands and only pausing occasionally to scan her surroundings. But when a vehicle rumbled along the lane toward her, she looked up and shaded her eyes from its headlights, opening her mouth in a grimace as she did so and revealing inflamed gums and missing teeth.

The car's lights illuminated her grimy face and bent figure in the stained, over-sized hoody that hung to her knees. Some of her matted grey dreadlocks had been caught in the rough texture of the hessian sack draped over her clothes – for additional warmth no doubt – while the rest of her hair hung greasily to her shoulders. Her lips moved in silent complaint as she watched the car, a 'nebula-gray pearl' Lexus sporting the flashy personal number plate *Mishrah,* pull up at the rear of the nightclub.

As soon as the car came to a stop, two men in black suits emerged from the front seats. One moved to stand by the rear of the vehicle, while the other took up position at the nightclub's back entrance. Once in place they nodded to each other and pulled pistols from inside their suit jackets, as the car's rear door opened and a smartly dressed man stepped out, straightening his tailor-made black pinstriped suit.

Despite the lane's dimness, the man wore mirrored aviator sunglasses. When he turned, the glow of the car's interior light revealed him to be dark-haired, with a fashionably stubbled jawline and a black tattoo on his neck.

A tattoo in the shape of a snake.

A black mamba.

'Wait for me,' a throaty voice called from inside the car. A hand with long, crimson fingernails gripped the open door, as a heavily made-up face below a mane of red hair appeared. 'Give me a hand, Suman?'

Suman.

Suman Mishrah.

The man gave an impatient huff and turned to help the buxom woman from the vehicle. Even with his arm around her waist her movements were awkward, hampered by her three inch stilettos and skin-tight leather miniskirt. The couple began shuffling their way around the car, followed by the guard, when a raspy voice emerged from the shadows.

'A dollar, can you spare a dollar?'

All three turned toward the voice to see the hunched-over bag lady materialise out of the gloom. She gave a guttural cough, hocked up a loogie and spat on the ground. 'A cigarette?' she rasped, 'for a poor old lady down on her luck?'

Mishrah's lips twisted with disgust and he jerked his chin at the guard, who pointed his Beretta at the bag lady's head and snarled, 'I ain't got a cigarette and you ain't no lady.' Screwing up his nose, he stepped in close to press the pistol against her forehead. 'Now get lost you old hag, you stink.'

He gave a start when, instead of recoiling as expected, the bag lady grabbed hold of his arm, deflecting his weapon. Using her free hand to pull a Walther PPQ from beneath her garb, she pressed the pistol's silencer snugly under the guard's chin … and pulled the trigger. She crouched, using his slumping body as a shield, and then, *blat!* she took out the guard standing at the rear of the nightclub.

The redhead flinched as the muffled shots rang out. She shrank back with a yelp, her eyes widening in fear and horror. Beside her, Mishrah sprang forward. Kicking the pistol out of the bag lady's hand with one foot, he used the other to stomp her in the side, forcing her to the ground.

She rolled backward onto her shoulders, placed her palms on the ground by her head and then, bringing up her legs and arching her back, thrust herself forward and onto her feet, just as Mishrah pulled a gold-plated, point fifty calibre Desert Eagle from the inside of his suit jacket. But before he could level the weapon, she kicked it out of his hand with her right foot and followed up with a round-house kick to his temple with her left. His head snapped sideways and he spun one-eighty degrees, falling face-down across the front of the Lexus.

While the redhead stood frozen, watching with wide, disbelieving eyes, hands clamped tightly across her mouth, the bag lady closed in. Mishrah remained lying across the bonnet, but surreptitiously reached a hand inside his jacket. As soon as his assailant was within arm's reach, he whipped around and lashed out.

The bag lady leapt back as the wickedly curved blade of a Nepalese kukri sailed past her throat with mere millimetres to spare. Rebounding a split second later she sprang toward him, blocking the return swing from his kukri arm and punching her clenched fist into his larynx. Still blocking his arm, she grabbed hold of his wrist and shoved her knee upward and into his groin.

This elicited the response she wanted.

As he gave an agonised gasp and doubled over, she caught the kukri as it fell from his hand and then spun back outward, coming to a stop holding the blade in a raised hand behind her and with her other arm forward in a defensive stance.

The redhead screamed as she watched Mishrah sag to the ground, hands at his throat as blood spurted from a deep three inch cut.

The bag lady watched him fall before relaxing and retrieving her pistol. Tugging off the stained mittens, she snapped on a pair of surgical gloves and proceeded to rifle through Mishrah's pockets as he lay gurgling his last breaths. The quivering redhead merely gaped down at them, her face crumpling and a howl forming in her throat.

Glancing up at her and yelling, 'Get lost!' the bag lady grabbed the Lexus keys from the pocket of the guard lying next to Mishrah. Picking up the Desert Eagle, she threw it onto the passenger's seat and then jumped behind the wheel. She reversed the Lexus out of the lane with a roar, passing the now wailing redhead as she went. With a squeal of tyres at the end of the lane, the prestige vehicle accelerated into the traffic and became just another car on busy Marsden Street.

After crossing the Parramatta River, the bag lady nosed the Lexus into a bay next to a park in Prince Alfred Square and switched off the engine. She paused, listening for a long moment. When all was quiet bar the normal late night city sounds, she peeled off the hessian bag and hoody. Taking a large plastic garbage bag from a pocket in her pants, she unfolded it and shoved the hoody and hessian bag into it. Then she reefed the wig of dreadlocks from her head and raked vigorous fingers through her own hair. Glancing in the rear view mirror, she unclipped the costume false teeth and threw them into the bag along with the wig.

Freed of her disguise, she took a second to glance outside, making sure her surroundings were clear of curious eyes, and then turned her attention to the car's interior. Among the contents of the unlocked glove box she found a pile of papers including the vehicle's registration certificate, made out to one Suman Mishrah. When a crumpled docket caught her eye, she smoothed it out and scanned the items listed on it – quantities of hydrochloric acid, ammonia hydroxide and sulphuric acid – all for delivery to a storage facility in Cecil Hills, east of Sydney.

Shoving the docket into a pants pocket, she returned the rest of the paperwork to the glove box and banged it shut. Glancing over at the passenger's seat, she picked up the Desert Eagle and felt its weight in her hand.

Nice weapon. Superior stopping power, but too bulky and heavy for my liking. Besides, a quick double tap with a nine mil gives roughly the same result.

Picking up the garbage bag, she slipped the Desert Eagle into it and got out of the vehicle. Now dressed in a khaki tee above black cargoes, she was a shadowy figure making her way along the path that skirted the park. She strode with purpose, head down, making straight for the midnight blue Kawasaki parked in the dimness by the curb.

After resting the garbage bag on the touring bike's wide seat, she tugged off the surgical gloves and tossed them into the bag with the other gear. Unlocking the Kawasaki's panniers, she took out a full-face helmet and replaced it with the garbage bag. From the other pannier she removed a slim-fit Rick Owen leather biker's jacket. Donning it and the helmet, she got on the bike and inserted the key in the ignition. As soon as she pressed the Start button the big bike roared into life, and an instant later was sailing her away from the scene of the triple homicide, bawling redhead, and gathering onlookers.

On the Pacific Motorway, heading toward the Gold Coast and home, Modeen pulled up on the bridge before Moonie Point and threw the garbage bag into the Hawkesbury River. She kept the motor running while watching the bag sink, and then accelerated back onto the freeway.

Yep, superior stopping power ... and a damn good anchor.

———

As she let herself into her apartment, her thoughts were already on her next trip to Hobart. Surely on this visit she'd find some improvement in Troy's condition – it was weeks now since that fatal Julia Creek mission.

But how long is a long time to be in a coma?

Pushing that worrying train of thought from her mind, she dropped her laptop on the foot of her queen-sized bed and switched it on. While it was booting up, she retrieved her cargo pants from the laundry hamper and dug in the pocket for the delivery docket she'd taken from Mishrah's Lexus. Unfolding it, she studied the details closely.

Hydrochloric acid, ammonia hydroxide and sulphuric acid, for delivery to Cecil Hills.

Cecil Hills.

The location of the warehouse to which the equipment from the Julia Creek meth lab had been consigned.

She gave a satisfied huff.

Except we cancelled that consignment.

Smoothing the docket with her hand, she mused, *it can't be a coincidence. That warehouse is a lead.*

She gave a decisive nod.

Definitely worth a stake-out when I get back from Hobart.

Opening the bottom drawer of her bedside table, she slipped the docket inside it and then removed the drawer to access the memory stick she'd taped behind the back of it. Plugging the stick into the laptop's USB port she opened a spreadsheet and clicked on a tab, and with a flourish, put a line through entry number eight, *Suman Mishrah.*

———

Taking her usual position beside Wolf on the hospital bed, she bent to kiss his forehead and took his nearest hand in hers. She smiled down at him and announced, 'I've brought you another Matthew Reilly book,' holding it up as if showing it to him. 'This one's called *Temple.'*

No response.

She lowered the book with a small sigh. Running her eyes over him, she took in the growing pallor of his normally tanned face, and the early signs of muscle wastage – atrophy the medical staff had called it – on his brawny arms.

Swallowing, she said brightly, 'The nurse says I can stay while you have your physiotherapy session today.' She opened the book to the first page. 'We'll start this and see how far we get, shall we?' Although posing it as a question, she wasn't expecting an answer. And the only response in the room was from the softly beeping monitors beside the bed.

With another small sigh, she cleared her throat and began to read.

Two orderlies bustled into the room carrying pieces of equipment. They nodded to Modeen, who rose and moved away from the bed to give them room.

One of the men smiled at her, saying jauntily, 'Just settin' 'im up for the Tour de France,' while the other flicked back the sheet and placed a modified cycling machine between Wolf's legs. They were strapping his feet and calves into the machine when the physiotherapist arrived. He watched the set-up closely, and when they'd finished he stepped in to manually cycle the machine, checking the action. With a dismissive nod at the orderlies, who promptly left, the physio switched on the machine and stood watching it for a few revolutions. Appearing satisfied, he turned and strode from the room with a brisk, 'See you in an hour,' to Modeen.

A modicum of quiet returned to the room. She remained standing, watching the machine revolve slowly, pumping Wolf's solid – if presently useless – legs while he lay on his back, oblivious to what was going on.

Putting a hand to her mouth, she gave a sad shake of her head.

He'd hate this ... being so helpless, so pitiable.

She pulled a chair closer to the bedside and sat in it with her head bent, gathering herself, before looking up at him with a shaky smile. 'Well, I guess it's safe for me to go on reading while you're—'

Her mobile gave a sudden buzz and vibrated. Pulling it from a back pocket, she glanced at the caller ID and pressed Answer.

'Hey Aunty Hann.'

'Hello love. How are you coping?' Although it sounded canned through the phone's speaker, Hannah Bourne's voice resonated with warmth and empathy.

'I'm OK,' Modeen replied in a low voice. 'How about you?'

'Just fine.' Her aunt's tone grew more perky. 'And I have a favour to ask.'

'Ask away.'

'Well, you see our writers' group has scheduled an info session on the Gold Coast, a follow-up from our recent conference, and I was wondering....'

Modeen gave a low chuckle. 'Sure Aunty Hann. You know you're always welcome to stay at my apartment, whether I'm there or not.'

'Thanks love.' Hannah paused before adding a tad awkwardly, 'And Richard...?'

'Salty?' Modeen smiled. 'He's welcome too.'

'Oh, that's wonderful dear! We arrive on Friday after-noon, hope that's OK?'

'I'll probably be down here in Hobart, but you can let yourselves in with the security code I gave you last time. Do you still have it?'

'Got it right here,' her aunt replied breezily. 'We're only staying a couple of days this time, and of course we'll leave the place pristine.'

'I know you will. And I hope you enjoy your stay and the writers' group session.'

'We will. And you take care, love,' Hannah said warmly, adding in a more sombre tone, 'And give that friend of yours my best, won't you?'

'I will.' Ending the call, Modeen glanced over at Wolf. 'Well, what d'you think about *that*? Seems my Aunty Hann and Salty are becoming quite the pair.'

CHAPTER SEVEN

After three days at Troy's bedside, longing to glimpse a flicker of recognition at the sound of her voice but seeing no change in his condition, Modeen's spirits plummeted. Marking time was something she'd grown accustomed to in the military, but she struggled to keep her restlessness and feelings of guilt in check during the hours and days spent waiting for signs of emerging consciousness. And while she waited, her memories tormented her with images from the ill-fated Julia Creek mission....

It was the last time she'd seen Troy conscious. Bending his helmet's mic arm closer to his mouth, he'd muttered, 'Wait 'til Bugs and I are in position before you approach the homestead.'

The four of them had just parachuted in, landing on a

patch of ground that was bare but for a speckling of low spinifex. With the faint sound of the military Taipan chopper fading to nothing in the night sky above them, the two snipers wove their way through the sparsely covered bush and disappeared from sight. They were tasked with providing cover as she and Spooky shut down operations of the super meth lab situated on the remote cattle station.

It was o-three hundred hours and the darkness was beginning to lift. Knowing the sun would rise in a couple of hours, she ordered Troy to take out the first guard.

Orders?

Who was she to give orders anyway?

They were all equally skilled soldiers….

In the hospital room she bent forward in the visitor's chair and put her head in her hands, trying not to dwell on the distressing thoughts and images, but her mind kept feeding them to her.

After setting the C4 charges and blowing the meth lab to hell, she'd heard Bugs' call for assistance when he found himself pinned down under heavy fire coming from the station's farmhouse. With Troy's position not allowing him to provide aid, she'd sprung into action, slamming a Kenworth prime mover into the hostiles hunkered down in the old Queenslander homestead.

She remembered standing on the roof of the prime mover after it had demolished the structure and seeing the R22 Robinson chopper in the sky above, with Reger at the stick. Then a triad of explosive charges had erupted along the eastern perimeter of the property. When the chopper was sent crashing to the south, she'd given a triumphant whoop … how that memory now stung …. and looked toward the rocky ridge where Troy was stationed. But her triumph evaporated when she saw Bugs break cover to sprint in the direction of the explosions.

Yelling into the comms, 'Bugs?' she heard him holler back, 'It's Wolf!'

Just two words, but they'd chilled her whole body.

Anxiously scanning ahead of Bugs, her gaze had fallen on the settling cloud of red dust.

And that's when she'd seen Troy's broken body lying among the rocks….

Leaping up from the visitor's chair, she paced the hospital room. She had to stop going over and over that scene or she'd go crazy. She needed to escape the miasma of frustrated uselessness … needed to *do* something … *accomplish* something.

And she knew what that something was.

First, she had to return home.

———

After a quick check of the delivery docket she'd taken from Mishrah's Lexus, she scrawled the address on a note and folded it into her camo cargos. Grabbing her partly packed duffel, she headed down the corridor to a small sunken room off the main hallway.

When presenting the Gold Coast apartment to his daughter as a gift – an unsolicited gift he'd hoped might encourage her to 'settle down', hopes he'd since relinquished – John Modeen had suggested the room would make an excellent wine cellar, perhaps even a nursery. She, however, had had other ideas.

In the centre of the compact space a Parabody G4 work station with leg press and double weight stack was flanked by a purpose-built dumbbell rack loaded with weights. Making her way behind the work station, she stopped in front of a shallow wall-mounted panel displaying an assortment of exercise gear. Around ninety centimetres wide by a metre and a half long, the panel had a skipping rope hanging down its left side and on the right, a selection of additional circular dumbbell weights on hooks.

Running a hand under the base of the panel's frame, she felt for the bolt-like handle. Grasping it with her fingers she pulled it to the right, and the left side of the panel popped forward. It swung open to reveal a shallow cavity containing empty gun racks.

Empty?

She frowned and sucked in her bottom lip.

Oh yeah, that's right. I had to return them to NatSec.

Closing the panel again, she turned and pressed the small black button at the back of the work station's weight tower. There was a solid clunk as the top step leading into the gym room jutted forward. She kneeled in front of it and pulled the step open. The deep, wide drawer rolled forward smoothly, revealing an assortment of rifles, handguns and other weapons, all resting snugly in custom-cut foam.

She opened her duffel and set it on the floor by her side. Reaching into the drawer, she retrieved a matt-black Walther PPQ. After checking the magazine she placed the pistol into the bag along with a spare clip, a box of nine millimetre cartridges, a pair of binoculars, and two remote spy cams.

In the basement carpark, she finished strapping the heavy duffel across the Kawasaki's rear seat and checked her watch.

Sixteen hundred hours.

Ahead of her was a five hour ride to Kempsey in northern New South Wales, her overnight stop. And the following morning an easy four and a half hour trip would see her at her destination.

The warehouse in Cecil Hills.

———

On the third level of Royal Hobart Hospital, H Block was a flurry of activity as the Assistant Nurses did their rounds. A young AN in one of the ward's private rooms glanced at her watch as she prepared to give yet another sponge bath. Ahead of schedule for a change, she was feeling on top of things. Humming a boppy tune, she pulled the curtains around the bed and used the remote control to raise the bed-head.

Once the comatose patient was at a forty-five degree angle, she unfastened the back of his hospital gown and let it drop to his waist. As she ran the sponge over his firm chest, she lifted the ring on the chain around his neck so she could wash his stubbled throat. Muttering, 'You could use a shave … *again,*' she grabbed a fresh white towel to dry him off and dropped the chain back onto his chest. Gazing down at it, she touched a finger to the ring. 'How come they left this on you?' Clicking her tongue, she said loftily, 'It only gets in the way.' Noting the glint of diamonds in the rose gold band, she took hold of the ring and cycled the chain through it until the latch appeared.

She was fumbling to unclip the latch when her wrist was suddenly grabbed. With a startled squeak she dropped the chain and jumped back, wrenching her hand free from the steely grip.

'What the—?' Rubbing her wrist, she stood breathing hard for a moment before rousing herself. Stepping forward, she grabbed the remote and pressed the Service button.

Less than a minute later a frowning Registered Nurse hurried into the room and barked, 'What is it?'

'He just grabbed my wrist!' The flushed AN pointed at the now still form on the bed.

The senior nurse's frown deepened. 'You sure?' Receiving a vigorous nod in reply, she turned her attention to the patient. Bending to peer into his face, she said crisply, 'Well then, it may not mean anything. Could've been just a reflex action.'

'I think it was more than—' The AN pulled up short at the sound of a low, rumbling groan from the bed.

The RN jerked upright and stared down at the patient. Turning on her heel, and with a meaningful glance at the wide-eyed AN, she barked, 'I'll alert the doctor,' and hurried from the room.

Leaning in close, the neurologist checked for pupil response with a small penlight. Next he clicked his fingers near the patient's left ear. When this met with a twitch away from the sound, he gave a brisk nod and announced, 'That's encouraging,' to the attentive RN at his side. Glancing down at the patient's chart, he clasped the hand nearest him and said in a firm voice, 'Can you squeeze my hand?'

No response.

'Troy, can you hear me?'

No response.

'Squeeze my hand, Troy.'

No response.

'Try touching the chain around his neck. That got him going before, when I went to take it off.' When her suggestion was ignored, the young AN stood on her toes, trying to see over the shoulders of her colleagues. Thinking of the patient's regular visitors she enquired eagerly, 'Shall I contact his next of kin?'

Her innocent enquiry earned her frowns from both the RN and the neurologist, who snapped, 'Emerging from a coma isn't like waking from regular sleep. It's too early to go raising their hopes.' He turned back to gaze down at Wolf. 'For now we'll just keep him under close observation.' He scrawled some notes on the chart and then strode from the room with a brusque, 'Call me if there's any significant change.'

Barking, 'Regular obs, nurse,' to the chagrined AN, the RN followed him out.

Close to the end of her shift, the AN called in to check on him one more time before knocking off for the evening. Finding everything quiet in the room, she was about to leave when out of the corner of her eye she caught movement on the bed. Whipping around, she saw her patient's arms twitch and then begin to flail by his sides. His eyes remained closed but his head jerked from side to side and his face twisted in a grimace. His breathing quickened and beads of sweat formed on his brow … but then seconds later he was still again.

The AN eyed him keenly, wondering if this latest episode qualified as a 'significant change'.

Not as significant as grabbing someone on the wrist, she mused wryly while diligently noting the incident details on the chart.

At the turn-off to the Motorway Motel in Kempsey, Modeen left the highway and parked the Kawasaki near the door to reception. A seventies-style motel, its accommodation blocks surrounded a courtyard and central carpark. Taking note of the empty bays in front of a number of the motel's units, she rang the night bell and heard footsteps on the floor above the office. Moments later the door opened and a balding older man squinted out at her.

'I'm booked in for tonight, name's Modeen,' she said pleasantly.

The man nodded. 'Right.'

'And I'd like to pay for the room now.'

'No problem.' The man opened the door wider and indicated for her to step inside. Behind the reception desk, he rummaged through a manila folder and came up with a check-in sheet which he slid across the counter to her. 'Just check the details and then sign at the bottom.'

As she took it and the proffered pen from him, he went on. 'And it'll be eighty bucks, thanks. That includes breakfast. You're in room twelve.' He reached under the desk and took out a key on a huge plastic tag, which he handed to Modeen. Lifting his chin at the Kawasaki ticking outside as it began to cool, he said gruffly, 'And our other guests would appreciate if you'd keep the noise down.'

'Noted.'

A short time later she opened the door to room twelve and stood in the doorway to take a quick scan. The place wasn't the Ritz, but it was clean and tidy and would do just fine for the night.

She took her time leaving the following morning, taking advantage of the 'included' continental breakfast which was delivered to her room at o-seven hundred.

An hour later she was checked out and standing by the bike, donning her helmet. About to hit the start button, she paused when her phone vibrated in the leg pocket of her cargos. Removing her helmet, she pulled out the mobile and put it to her ear.

'Hello?'

'Jo?'

'Yes.'

'Jake here.'

Her heart turned over in her chest.

Bad news?

At her silence he added tentatively, 'Troy's brother?'

She struggled to keep her tone even. 'Yes Jake?'

'I've got some good news.'

Her spirits rose.

'He's coming out of the coma,' Jake gushed. 'Opened his eyes at around six this morning.'

Her heart leapt into her throat and she blinked hard as he went on.

'The doc says his vision's blurry but it'll get better. Apparently that's common in these cases.'

Modeen took a deep, calming breath. 'That's *wonderful*, Jake! Has he said anything? Can he talk?'

'The nurse who rang me said his speech is slurred so it's hard to understand what he's trying to say, but the doc reckons his speech should improve too. I'm heading in as soon as I get off the phone. Will let you know how I get on.'

The smile in his voice had her smiling too, and his news eclipsed all thoughts of the Cecil Hills warehouse.

'Please do. And thanks so much for letting me know, Jake. I'm in Kempsey at present but will head straight home and arrange to be on the next flight to Hobart. All going well, I should be there late this afternoon.'

'Great.' Before signing off, Jake said cheerily, 'Troy'll be eager to see you.'

Just before the town of Woodburn her phone vibrated again. She hesitated to stop and lose time after having ridden hard, driven by the prospect of seeing Troy awake at last. But at the thought it might be Jake with an update, she pulled over to the verge and took the call, putting the phone to one ear while covering the other with her free hand to muffle the roar of vehicles on the busy highway.

'Hello?'

'Jo, it's Jake again.'

'Hey Jake. How's Troy doing?'

'His speech and eyesight are already improving. He told us he could make out our shapes in the room, and we understood what he was saying.' Jake paused and Modeen had the feeling she'd just been given the good news and was about to hear the bad. 'It seems his long term memory is OK … but his short term not so much.'

She frowned. 'Oh?'

'The doc's real happy with him and expects he'll continue to improve … but….' Jake paused again as if searching for the right words.

When he didn't speak for a long moment, Modeen prompted, 'But what, Jake?'

'He recognised me, but was surprised I looked so old.' He gave a humourless snort. 'Seems he's lost some of his short term memories. The doc says that's another common side effect of coming out of a coma, especially for a patient who's suffered severe head trauma. He reckons it could take days, weeks or even months for him to regain those later memories … although there's no guarantee that he'll get them all back.'

'I see.' Her voice was low, tense.

'And Jo….'

'Yes?'

'He … um … doesn't remember you. For now, that is.' Greeted with a stony silence, he went on hastily, 'I told him you were coming to see him, thinking he'd be excited—' He took a breath. 'I even used your full name but … he asked me who I was talking about, said he doesn't know a Jo Modeen. Don't stress about it though, he also doesn't remember being in the Special Forces.'

Lowering her head, she blinked and swallowed before saying in a strangled voice, 'The main thing is, he's awake and improving. Thanks for letting me know.' She took a breath. 'I'm a couple of hours from home. The minute I get there I'll book myself on the next available flight.'

'No problem, Jo,' Jake said kindly. 'See you when you get here.'

Jamming her finger on the End Call button, she shoved the phone back in the pocket of her cargos and kicked the bike into gear. Wrenching the throttle open, she dropped the clutch and the big bike roared back onto the highway with a rooster tail of gravel and a squeal of rubber on warm bitumen.

CHAPTER EIGHT

At thirteen hundred hours Modeen idled down the ramp and into the carpark in the basement of her apartment complex. The GTR's deep motor rumble resonated off the thick concrete walls as she nosed the bike into her designated parking bay. Dismounting, she stretched to loosen her travel-cramped muscles and then unstrapped her duffel from off the back of the bike before heading to the stairs.

Once in her apartment she dumped the duffel on the floor and flopped onto the couch to book the next available flight to Hobart on her mobile. That done, she took her bag into the master bedroom, removed the weaponry, and proceeded to repack it with extra clothes for the longer stay and a thick woollen jumper for Tassie's notoriously cold weather.

She checked her watch.

Just enough time to get in a shower and a quick bite before I head to the airport.

Feeling refreshed after her shower, and munching on a crisp apple, she locked her apartment and took the lift to the lobby.

While it enjoyed a prime location in Surfers Paradise, her apartment building's exterior was beginning to look dated amid the showy new high-rises going up around it with startling, investor-driven speed. Having been originally designed to cater for owner occupiers and long term residents, the building had a lobby that was a token at best, devoid of the glitz evident in dedicated tourist hotels and resorts. There was no reception desk for one thing, just a wall-mounted Perspex sign advising that the building superintendent resided on the first level, and to use the intercom button below the sign if requiring his services.

For another thing, the elevator didn't go all the way to the basement carpark. That level was accessed via two short flights of stairs and a disabled ramp, provided for the 'convenience' of the building's residents. This was a design flaw that sparked regular complaints from tenants, especially those with limited or obesity-affected agility, but one the body corporate was loath to even acknowledge. For an able body like Modeen the stairs were no burden, in fact she had used the climb as a pre-gym warm-up on many occasions.

She tripped lightly down them now and through the exit door into the basement, a smile tugging at her mouth at the thought of seeing Wolf finally awake. But as she turned to make her way to the GTR, the smile dissolved at the sight of a tall, solidly built man leaning casually against her bike. Stopping in her tracks, she took a quick sweep of the basement. Behind the man, about three bays back, a silver grey Ford Transit caught her eye.

I haven't seen that van in here before.

Fixing her gaze back on the man, she took in his dark-coloured V-neck tee shirt over a muscular chest and black denim jeans secured with a leather belt sporting a large silver buckle. He, in turn, looked her up and down and then grinned, his teeth showing white in his dark-skinned face. When her eyes fell on the tribal tattoos running from his right temple and down his neck, she dropped her duffel at her feet and took up a defensive stance.

A Black Mamba.

She swallowed.

They've found me.

THWACK!

The sharp jab in her right buttock made her gasp and jump forward, twisting to grab whatever it was that had struck her. But even as she yanked the offending item from her gluteus medius she felt a sting course into her body. She stared down at the item in her hand. The metal dart was roughly ten millimetres in diameter and twenty-five millimetres long, with a tuft of downy yellow feathers for a tail. Scowling, she let it slip from her fingers and whirled around to face the direction it had come from, ignoring the sudden onset of dizziness that accompanied the abrupt move.

Three dark-skinned men swaggered from the dimly lit confines of the basement, one with a tranquilliser rifle resting on a beefy shoulder. They stopped a short distance away from her and the smallest of the three elbowed his rifle-wielding mate. 'Nice shot,' he said jauntily.

Modeen blinked hard, trying to stay focused, trying to resist the waves of numbness creeping up and over her. Seeing her tilt and take a staggering step to the side, the nearest man moved in to grab her. At his approach she shook her head and the fog cleared momentarily. Curling beneath his outstretched arm, she used a Judo throw to hurl him over her shoulder. He gave a surprised bellow and then hit the concrete with an explosive grunt as the air was punched from his lungs.

The guy with the tranquilliser rifle lowered the weapon from his shoulder and stepped in, intending to jab her in the head with the rifle's butt. Gathering her diminishing wits with a force of will, she knocked the man's leading leg to the side with a sweep of her right foot, unbalancing him. As he struggled to remain upright, she sent him to the concrete with a round-house kick to the side of the head, rifle clattering uselessly to the floor beside him.

The man leaning on her bike straightened and took a

couple of steps toward her. At the same time the last of the three men moved in and grabbed her in a bear hug. He received an elbow in the face for his troubles and gave a pained grunt, but managed to keep hold of her. So when she sagged sideways, eyes rolling back and legs turning to jelly beneath her, he took her weight and then scooped her into his arms, puffing, 'I guess that's why the Boss wanted her sedated.'

The man with the silver buckle grinned and jerked his head toward the Ford Transit van. 'Put 'er in the back and make sure she's secure. We don't want 'er getting loose.' He looked across at the other sour-faced goons who were picking themselves up off the floor. 'C'mon you idiots.' He pointed to the ground near them. 'And don't forget the rifle.'

Sitting up front with the driver, he tapped on his mobile phone and a few seconds later announced, 'The jetty, ninety minutes.' Ending the call he glanced into the back of the van where Modeen lay out cold, her hands and ankles bound and a pillowslip secured over her head. 'Didja check 'er pockets?'

The two goons in the back patted her down. When one of them lingered over the job, leering down at her, the man in the front growled, 'Don't muck around. I want us out of here, pronto.'

The goon sat back, raising his hands as if in surrender, while his counterpart held up a mobile phone and a thin wallet with a satisfied flourish.

When the man in the front barked, 'Hand me the

wallet and ditch the phone,' the goon passed the wallet forward then promptly opened the sliding door to fling the mobile out. It hit the basement's concrete wall, smashing into pieces. With a satisfied grunt the man with the silver buckle turned to the front again as the van's door slid closed. He flicked through the wallet with a smug half grin and then lifted his chin at the driver. 'Go!'

The two goons in the back kept their eyes on the unconscious Modeen and braced themselves as the van powered up the exit ramp and headed for the M1 Motorway.

———

In Royal Hobart Hospital, Ben Logan stopped at the doorway of a private room and looked in. He saw Jake Wolverton at his brother's bedside. Troy Wolverton was sitting upright and appeared to Ben to be reasonably alert for someone who'd only that morning emerged from a coma. When Jake acknowledged him with a nod, Ben returned the greeting and stepped into the room to make his way to the other side of the bed.

'Wolf.' He smiled and extended a hand. 'Good to see you awake.'

Wolf stared up at his visitor's impressive six foot four physique and frowned. He was used to being called Wolf; it had been his nickname since school days and was an obvious shortening of his surname. In addition to that, he liked it. But who was this person using it so naturally? He took Ben's extended hand and shook it. 'Thank you.' He indicated Jake with a bob of his head. 'This is my brother, Jake. And you are?'

Ben glanced at Jake. 'Good to see you again.'

'Likewise.' Jake threw him a look of apology for his brother's terseness.

Ben turned back to Wolf, his expression serious. 'I'm your commanding officer. Name's Ben Smith.'

Still eyeing him, Wolf drawled, 'My CO? So why the civvies?'

Ben glanced down at his charcoal grey suit and then back at Wolf. 'We're part of a special ops unit. When we're not on a mission we dress in civvies. Besides, I'm not here in an official capacity; I'm here as a friend.'

'A friend?' Wolf raised one dark eyebrow and growled, 'Well then maybe you can tell me what the *hell* happened to me and how the *hell* I got here?' He stabbed the air with an agitated hand to indicate the hospital room. Lowering his arm again and scowling at Jake, he went on. ''Cos my brother here either doesn't know or isn't sayin'.'

Ben threw Jake a sympathetic glance and then looked back at Wolf. 'You don't remember what happened?'

'No.' Deep furrows appeared in Wolf's brow. He dragged a hand over his face before saying hesitantly, 'What Jake *did* tell me is … that I've been in the SASR for about five years.' His frown deepened. 'But I don't remember any of that.' He stared up at Ben again. 'And you don't look familiar.'

'What Jake's told you is correct.' Ben put a comforting hand on Wolf's shoulder. 'I met you in the SASR, we joined around the same time.'

'That doesn't explain why I'm in *here*.'

'You were on a mission when you were injured.'

'What sort of mission?'

Seeing Jake's warning glance and recalling the neurologist's advice, Ben said carefully, 'It was classified; but you don't need to worry about that now. What you need to focus on is resting up and giving yourself time to recover.' Taking a NatSec mobile phone out of a pocket, he handed it to Wolf. 'My number's the only one in the contacts list. You can call me any time.'

'Thanks … I guess.' Gazing quizzically at Ben, Wolf took the phone from him.

Ben nodded and then glanced at Jake. 'Has JD … I mean Jo … arrived yet?'

Jake shook his head. 'Haven't seen her, but then she wasn't specific about a time. I figured it was an even bet which one of you would get here first.'

Pulling out his own mobile, Ben excused himself and went to the corner of the room. He tapped on the touch screen and zoomed in on a small green dot on the Gold Coast. His eyes narrowed.

She's either still at her apartment or has left her tracker behind.

He swiped the screen and brought up his contacts list. Tapping on her number, he listened to it ring a few times and then her voice came on.

'This is Jo. Leave your name and number and I'll get back to you.'

He gave a frustrated exhalation. 'JD, it's Ben. Call me back ASAP,' and then closed his mobile's case with a snap. Re-joining Jake and Wolf, he said gruffly, 'She's not answering … maybe 'cos she's in transit.'

'You talkin' about Jo?'

Ben brightened. 'You remember her, Wolf?'

'No.' Wolf frowned. 'But from the bits Jake's told me I feel like I should.'

Leaning down, Ben lifted the chain from beneath Wolf's hospital gown. When the ring came free he held it out, shooting Wolf a significant glance, before dropping the chain again. 'What's the last thing you remember?'

Staring at Ben with questions in his dark eyes, Wolf replied slowly, 'I remember signing up for the Regulars. I remember being in Afghanistan at a posting north of Tarin Kowt, but nothing after that.'

'What unit were you with in the Middle East?'

Wolf eyed Ben and said proudly, 'The Seventh Battalion, Royal Australian Regiment.'

'Do you remember a soldier named Luke Jackson?'

'Spooky Luke? Sure, he was in the Sixth. A damn good tracker and point-man if I remember right. Why do you ask?'

'He was on the team with you when you were wounded. I let him know you've regained consciousness and he's planning to pay you a visit in the next couple of days.'

'Next couple of days?' Wolf growled. 'I'll be *out* of here in the next couple of days.'

'It's too early to be even contemplating that, Mr Wolverton.' The three men looked toward the doorway as the neurologist entered the room. 'You need to undergo some strenuous physiotherapy before you go anywhere. And right now, you need to rest.'

When the doctor took the clipboard from the base of the bed and flicked over the top sheet to study the notations on the chart, Ben turned to Jake. 'I'm staying in the city. Don't hesitate to call me if you need anything.'

'Thanks.' Jake nodded. 'And thanks for everything you've done already.'

Dipping his head at Jake, Ben turned to give Wolf's shoulder a thump. 'See you tomorrow, mate.' As he passed the doctor on his way out of the room Ben said crisply, 'And I'll see you tomorrow for that follow-up report.'

'I'll be here, Mr Smith. Just ask the ward nurse to page me.'

The late model silver grey Ford Transit turned right onto the six lane motorway and headed north, its V6 engine easily powering the van to the highway's speed limit of one hundred and ten kilometres per hour. Merging with the thickening traffic of the evening's rush hour, the van cruised past Helensvale and Coomera and then took the off-ramp which circled over the M1 motorway at Pimpama.

In the front seat, the man with the silver buckle made another call on his mobile. He turned on the speaker function and spoke down at the phone, the Kiwi accent in his deep voice unmistakeable. 'We've secured the package, boss, and are headin' for the transport.'

'Good,' came the drawled reply. 'Is the package undamaged?'

'Yeah.' The man swallowed a grin. 'Bar a little pin prick in the butt.'

'Good,' the voice said again. 'Keep it that way.'

'Will do, boss.' Ending that call, the man tapped on another number and moments later said sharply, 'What's your ETA?'

'We should be there just on dusk.'

'Right. We're on Jacob Wells Road heading for Woongoolba.' The man with the silver buckle snapped his phone closed and nodded to the driver.

As the sun sank low on the horizon, a fifteen metre-long steel prawn trawler chugged through the heads between North and South Stradbroke Islands. With her enormous outriggers, the *North Island Star* made an impressive silhouette against the waning daylight. After negotiating her way through Tipplers Passage, the trawler slowed as she approached the mainland jetty at the end of Steiglitz Road.

As the silver-grey Transit van pulled up at the jetty's security gate, its headlights illuminated the trawler's white cabin and blue hull. The driver flashed the lights to signal those aboard the boat as the man with the silver buckle got out of the van holding a pair of bolt cutters. After slicing through the padlock securing the gates he pushed them open, and then jogged behind the van as it drove through the gateway and came to a stop at the jetty. The side door of the van slid open and the two goons in the back jumped out and stretched.

The man lifted his chin at them and ordered, 'Put 'er in the front cargo hold,' pointing at the trawler. Then he circled around to the driver's side and tapped on the window. As it buzzed down, he handed the driver an envelope but kept hold of one side of it while staring into the other man's eyes. 'You saw nothing,' he growled, 'you heard nothing, and you were never here. Right?'

At the driver's murmured, 'Right,' the man with the sliver buckle let go of the envelope and stepped back. 'Now get out of here.'

As the van accelerated away in a shower of gravel the three men strode onto the jetty, only just discernible in the dimming daylight. To a keen-eyed observer it was clear one of them carried a limp body in his arms. A body with curves whose head was covered and whose wrists and ankles were bound. But there were no observers, the man with the silver buckle had made sure of that.

Toward the front of the trawler, in a tiny cabin which

had been stripped bare save for a well-worn bunk bed and corner portable toilet, her captors laid Modeen on the bunk and then left, locking the door behind them. On deck, standing in the lightly salted breeze, the man with the silver buckle paused to watch the van continue powering away from the compound. Satisfied all was as it should be, he turned toward the trawler's wheelhouse and called to the captain to get under way.

CHAPTER NINE

On the rear deck of his multi-level hillside home, Richard Salt leaned back in the tall outdoor chair, eyes crinkling in the corners as he swept a glance over the inlet and Port Douglas township below. He never tired of the commanding view. Stretching out his darkly tanned legs, he rested his feet on the balustrade's top rail and twisted the cap off an icy stubby of beer. Smiling at the promising hiss of escaping effervescence from the brown glass bottle, he raised the chilled beer to his lips … only to pause and scowl when the mobile phone on the table beside him buzzed.

He sighed, took a long swig from the stubby, and picked up the phone. As soon as he pressed Answer, a deep voice said, 'Salty?' He exhaled, recognising the caller and knowing this would not be a social call. 'Yeah, Ben.'

'I need someone on the Gold Coast ASAP,' Ben Logan said crisply, 'someone I can trust. You available?'

Salty's ears picked up the thread of tension in Ben's voice. He frowned but kept his tone light when he said, 'I'm fine, Youngster, thanks for askin'.' Hearing an impatient exhalation at the other end of the line, he hastened to add, 'And as it so happens, I'm headin' to Surfers Paradise in a coupl'a days.'

'I need someone there *now*. Any chance you could arrange to be on the next flight down?'

Salty took another swig of beer before enquiring, 'You've got an agent there, why not use her?' His eyes narrowed. 'Modeen's still on the Gold Coast isn't she?'

'This request … isn't sanctioned and I want to keep it low key.' Ben paused before saying slowly, 'Besides … it's JD I need you to check on.'

Muttering drily, 'How about you lead with that next time,' Salty sat upright. 'Now, what's happened?'

'I've lost contact with her. She was supposed to be on her way to Hobart, but as far as I can tell she never made it to the airport for her flight. I'm concerned for her safety.'

'One of its agents has dropped off the radar,' Salty said, his tone rising with incredulity, 'and NatSec hasn't sanctioned an investigation?'

Ben sighed and Salty could picture him running an agitated hand over his head. 'It's a long story. You just need to trust me.'

'I see. Well then, I'm on my way to the airport.'

Draining the stubby, Salty sprang to his feet and headed inside to the bedroom, phone still pressed to his ear. 'I'll try for a direct flight to Coolangatta, but I'll take whatever's the quickest option.'

'Thanks mate, I'll fill you in on the details when I can.' The relief was obvious in Ben's tone. 'I'll cover your costs so keep track of your expenses. And I'll text you JD's address in Surfers Paradise as soon as I'm off this call.'

'No need,' Salty said crisply, 'I've got it already.'

'Oh?'

'Yeah, I was gonna be stayin' there.' At the silence that followed that statement, Salty explained, 'With her aunty Hannah. She's a fellow scribbler; we're attending a writing session together. She won't be there for a coupl'a days though.'

'Right. Well, as soon as you get there, contact me with a sit-rep. I'll be waiting for your call.'

'Will do, Ben.' Tossing the mobile onto the bed, Salty dragged out his suitcase.

The *North Island Star* chugged back through the heads between North and South Stradbroke islands, the bow of its five-and-a-half metre wide hull climbing and falling with increasing intensity in the rising swell. When it fell against a wave with a resounding crash, Modeen gasped and jerked awake in the front cabin. She went to sit up only to fall back against the bunk, her head woozy from the tranquillising agent's lingering effects. Blinking hard, she peered into the cabin's thick darkness.

When no forms emerged, she began to wonder if her eyes were in fact open. But the rocking of her bunk, nearby slapping of water, the taste of salt on her tongue, and the heavy smell of fish on the air left her in no doubt that she was on a boat.

She raised a hand, only to find it bound to her other wrist in front of her. Lifting them both, she touched her face and was relieved when she felt fabric. She sat up slowly and tugged the covering off her head, flinging it to the floor. Blinking, she peered around, but her surroundings remained shrouded in darkness. Frustrated, she slumped back against the bunk.

In the trawler's wheelhouse above, the captain was busy with a nautical map and a pair of callipers. When the man with the silver buckle sauntered in to stand beside him the captain announced, 'We're averaging ten knots.'

'So how long 'til we get there?'

'Twenty-three hundred kilometres....' The captain rubbed his stubbled chin with a greasy hand. 'If we maintain this speed, we should be there in … about five days.'

With a gruff, 'Right,' the man with the silver buckle turned and strode out again.

———

At twenty-two hundred hours Salty fronted up to the nearest car rental counter in the Brisbane airport terminal, parking his two-wheeled carry-on suitcase by his side and smiling at the young woman manning the counter. She flicked an amused glance over the darkly tanned, silver-haired man in the blue safari suit, noting an aroma of wardrobe camphor about him, and returned his smile.

'Can I help you, sir?'

Half an hour later he was in a white Hyundai i20 heading south on the Gateway Motorway toward the Gold Coast. And an hour after that the i20 sat in a parking bay, ticking as it cooled, in front of Modeen's apartment building. Sitting back in the driver's seat, Salty scanned the immediate area.

Nothing out of the ordinary.

He checked his watch.

Almost midnight.

Unclipping his seatbelt, he slipped out of the car and strolled casually to the apartment building's entrance. Stopping near the front door, he took a quick look around, ears pricked for any unusual sounds. Satisfied all was quiet, he keyed in the security code Modeen's aunty Hannah had given him. When the door slid open, he took another quick check of his immediate surroundings before entering the building. He took the lift, and once outside her penthouse apartment stood close to the door and pressed an ear against it.

Nothing, not a sound.

He tried the door handle.

Locked.

Reaching into the inside pocket of his jacket, he pulled out a black leather satchel. Taking out two small metal pick-like tools, he went to work on the lock. In less time than it should have taken, he had jimmied it open.

But then I have been trained in these types of skills, even if it was a while ago. He gave a silent snort. *While your average crim is more opportunistic than competent.*

He stepped inside, taking care to move silently, eyes peeled for any movement. For an older man his night vision was still surprisingly good, and the moonlight shining through the open curtains provided enough light for him to make his way in the dimness. His familiarity with the layout, having stayed there before, was also helpful.

Once certain he was alone in the apartment he switched on the lights and began a proper, and extensive, search of the premises.

It was one-thirty am before he made the call to Ben. Despite the early hour, his call was answered on the second ring.

'Salty?'

'Yep. Thought you'd wanna know there's nothin' much to report here. Nobody watchin' the building and the apartment is neat and tidy, no sign of a scuffle. The only things I've found of interest is a docket for delivery of chemicals to a Cecil Hills location, for one Suman Mishrah. That, and a USB memory stick that was taped to the back of a drawer in the main bedroom.'

'What sort of chemicals were on the docket?'

Salty unfolded the crumpled receipt and read out the list. 'Hydrochloric acid, ammonia hydroxide and sulphuric acid.' He folded the docket again. 'If I'm not mistaken, these are common ingredients used for cookin' up a batch of meths.'

Ben gave a grunt and Salty's ears strained to hear his muttered, 'Why am I not surprised.' Clearing his throat, Ben went on tersely, 'Anything interesting on the memory stick?'

'Haven't been able to check. I've got Modeen's computer here but it's password protected.'

'What about her duffel? Is it in the apartment?'

'No sign of it.'

At the other end of the call, Ben tapped his mobile's screen and brought up a tracking app. He zoomed in on two green dots on the Gold Coast and announced, 'I'm picking up her tracker. It's approximately fifteen metres north of your location.'

From where he stood in the apartment's master bedroom, Salty looked out the glass doors at the ocean and then left, toward north. He frowned. 'Hang on.' Unlocking the sliding door, he stepped out onto the balcony and went to the balustrade. Looking down, he murmured, 'Fifteen metres north you say?'

'Yep.'

'That's gotta be in the basement carpark.' Straightening, he turned on his heel and strode back inside. 'I'll head down there now.'

Exiting the elevator on the lobby level, he took the stairs to the basement. The security roller door at the entrance of the carpark was down, and the night lights cast shadows around the subterranean pillars supporting the building's high-rise structure.

Hearing Ben's voice coming from the mobile in his hand, he raised it and pressed it to his ear again. 'What was that?'

'I said turn right,' Ben barked. 'Should be just in front of you about eight metres away.'

Salty squinted and announced, 'It's her motorcycle.' Then, 'Hang on,' as he glimpsed something on the ground beside it. He moved closer. 'Her duffel's here too.' Squatting by the bike he opened the bag. 'It's pretty full … looks like she'd packed to be away a while.'

'Anything else?' As he spoke Ben brought up another app on his phone, while Salty scanned the immediate area for anything out of place.

After a minute Salty said in a voice loaded with concern, 'I've found a phone. Looks to've been smashed against the wall near the carpark's exit ramp. It's been busted up pretty bad.'

'Make sure you get all of it,' Ben said brusquely. 'And do you still have the USB stick?'

'Yep.'

'Good. I want you to stay in the building. I'm going to wake the Super and get him to retrieve the footage from the camera outside the carpark. He's bound to have a computer. You can use it to view the data on the stick.'

Salty's lips twitched at the thought of the sleepy Super being roused by a forceful Ben, who wouldn't take no for an answer. He said quietly, 'I thought you wanted to keep this low key?' and heard Ben exhale.

'Your findings have confirmed my fears.' He sighed. 'JD's been abducted. And as she was a NatSec agent this becomes a national security issue, which means I'm authorised to allocate resources.'

Salty frowned. 'Did you say she *was* an agent?'

'I'll fill you in when I can. For now, sit tight. After I've spoken to the Super, I'll send an agent to pick up the delivery docket and JD's mobile from you. You OK to stay in her apartment in the meantime?'

'Sure. And you'll keep me posted?'

'Will do. And thanks, Salty.' With those words, Ben was gone.

Back in the lobby a short time later, Salty heard the elevator ping and looked toward it. A bleary-eyed, tousle-haired man in a white singlet and baggy tracksuit pants burst out of the lift, hastily looking to left and right. His eyes widened when they fell on Salty.

'Hey!' he called, 'you Richard Salt?' His voice was shrill with trepidation.

Knowing Ben had that effect on some people, especially when he was on a mission, Salty glanced around at the foyer, which was empty save for himself and the Super. He grinned. 'That would be me.'

'C-could you come with me, please?' The man beckoned him urgently and stepped back into the elevator.

When Salty joined him, the Super hit the button to the first floor. As the elevator began its climb, he stared at Salty, taking in his old-fashioned clothing and obvious age. 'So … you're really National Security?' At Salty's nod, he went on. 'Can your Mr Smith really do what he said?'

Salty swallowed a grin. 'What did he say he'd do?'

'Have this place crawling with local and federal police if I didn't comply.'

Eyeing the clearly nervous Super, Salty said slowly, 'Let's just say … he has a lot of resources at his disposal.' The other man blanched and stared at him, mouth agape. When the lift pinged its arrival, Salty clapped the startled Super on the shoulder. 'But you're a smart man,' he said reassuringly, 'so I'm sure he won't need to use them. Now let's get that video footage and see what all this fuss is about, shall we?'

CHAPTER TEN

In the early morning dimness of his Hobart hotel room, Ben sat staring at his laptop's screen. He scanned the footage that the sleepy and at first reluctant, but later eagerly accommodating, building super had retrieved from the surveillance camera focused on the front of Modeen's apartment building. His eyes darted around the screen as he familiarised himself with the locale, every now and then pausing, rewinding and reviewing so he could determine what was normal activity and what wasn't.

Always on the look-out for anything out of the ordinary.

And he knew he'd found it when a pale-coloured van flashed across the screen, exiting the basement carpark at speed.

Pausing the video, he checked the time stamp – sixteen forty-five the previous day. He took a screen dump of the image, saved it to his computer's desktop and then zoomed in on the vehicle's number plate to take another screen dump of it alone. Returning to the footage, he pressed the fast rewind key and saw the vehicle 'reverse' into the basement in fast motion. With eyes glued to the screen, he kept his finger on the rewind key and watched an innocuous-looking mid-sized sedan enter the basement and an equally innocuous two door hatch exit it.

And then the pale van appeared again, this time reversing out of the basement and onto the road. Freezing the frame, Ben glanced at the time stamp – fourteen seventeen – and saved a screen dump of the image. He pressed the play button to watch the van in real time turn off Ferry Avenue and into the apartment building's driveway. Pausing the footage again, he zoomed in on the windscreen until he could see the van's occupants.

Two large men filled – make that overflowed – the van's front bucket seats. Both wore serious, intent expressions on their broad, dark-skinned faces.

Maoris, of that he was certain.

Grabbing his phone, Ben scrolled through his contacts list and clicked on the number for James O'Neill. His call was answered after a few rings.

'IT,' a drowsy voice said, 'this is James.'

'I'm sending you some photos of a silver-grey Ford Transit van. It arrived at the Capricorn Two apartments in Surfers Paradise on Ferry Avenue at fourteen seventeen yesterday and left at sixteen forty-five, heading south. I want you to access the Transport and Main Roads street and highway cameras and find out where the van went. Track it as far as you can and give me a run-down of its movements.'

At the other end of the line NatSec's IT guru's voice still sounded nasal but with a sharper note, as though he'd sat up in bed to clear the last vestiges of slumber from his mind. 'No worries Ben, but it could take quite a few hours.'

'Just get me those details quick as you can,' Ben said brusquely. 'I'm in Hobart at present and can be reached on my mobile.'

'Will do.'

As soon as he ended that call, Ben made another. 'Bugs, I need you in Sydney ASAP.'

In his Canberra inner city apartment, NatSec agent Barry Peterson sat up in bed, blinking and rubbing a large hand over his strawberry-blonde buzz-cut. 'No problem Ben,' he said thickly. 'What's the assignment?'

'I want you to check out a warehouse in Cecil Hills. The place is called Green Hills Storage, on Tattersall Road. I'll text you the details.'

'Sure.' Ben heard him take a deep inhalation and then there were sounds of movement, as though he'd risen to his feet. 'No problem.'

'Bugs.'

At the urgent note in Ben's voice, Bugs stopped what he was doing and frowned. 'Yeah?'

'JD's gone missing.'

'Missin'?'

'Yes, and this warehouse may provide a lead as to her whereabouts.'

After a long moment Bugs barked, 'Understood,' and then, 'Cecil Hills? Isn't that where the lab equipment from the Julia Creek raid was headed?'

'Correct. I believe JD was doing some of her own....' Ben paused, searching for the right words. '... follow-up research, and I believe this may have led to her disappearance.'

Glancing at his watch, Bugs said flatly, 'It'll take me about two and a half hours. Should be there around mid-mornin'.'

'Right. And I have some good news as well. Wolf regained consciousness yesterday. I'm going to the hospital this morning to look in on him.'

'That's terrific!'

'Yeah, it is.' Ben shook his head and sighed. 'Except now JD's gone missing.'

'Well … shit!' Bugs swore some more under his breath. 'Talk about rotten timing! She was really holdin' out to see him wake up.'

Neither men spoke for a long moment and then Bugs said in a reassuringly confident tone, 'Don't worry, Ben, we'll find 'er. And say g'day to the wolfman for me.'

'Shall do.'

———

The *North Island Star* chugged through the gentle early morning swell. Modeen lay on her bunk in the cramped cabin, hands behind her head, breathing in the salt-laden air and listening to the pleading squawk of seagulls hovering just above the waves outside.

Troy….

She chewed her lip.

Did he wake up whole, as his old self?

Does he remember me … us?

Is he wondering why I'm not there with him?

Above her cabin, she heard the wheelhouse door open and close again. Then came heavy footsteps as someone went to the railing and threw scraps to the waiting gulls, whose pleading squawks turned into belligerent protests as the birds dived on the handouts *en masse*.

At the jingle of keys outside the cabin door, Modeen sprang to her feet. The door rattled and then swung open, allowing a stream of light to cut through the room's dimness. Almost immediately a large figure entered the doorway, blocking the light. Trying not to tip the bowl he carried in both hands, the man stepped tentatively over the raised ridge at the foot of the door, squinting as his eyes adjusted to the low light.

Leaping at him sideways from out of the gloom, Modeen grabbed his nearest hand and jerked him past her, elbowing him in the side of the head as he lost his footing and careered off balance. As he tumbled heavily to the bunk, the steaming bowl flew out of his hands to slam into the bulkhead, splattering its contents. Sliding down the wall on a wave of porridge, the bowl finally clattered to rest on the floor.

Without hesitation Modeen slipped through the open doorway and into a larger common room. She squinted as the sun glinted off the water and through a nearby porthole, stinging her eyes. She paused briefly to get her bearings. The wheelhouse was directly above the cabin, of that she was certain.

And that was where she would head first.

At a slight commotion to her left she whirled around. The red beam of a laser sight sliced through the air and *thwack!* two silver electrodes struck her in the midsection. Her body went rigid as fifty-five thousand volts at point zero zero five amps threw every muscle into violent contraction. Her brain told her she had been Tasered, but the electrical current flowing through it, and the excruciating pain accompanying it, rendered her body completely unresponsive to her commands.

After what felt to her like an agonising two minutes but was in fact only five seconds, the man with the silver buckle released the trigger of the X26C weapon. He watched Modeen slump to the floor like a rag doll and gave a disdainful, 'Humph.' Turning to the two crew members standing behind him, he barked, 'Restrain her *properly* this time.' He tossed them a pair of handcuffs and a length of chain. 'Secure her to the bulkhead with just enough slack to reach the loo.'

'Yes boss.'

The man lifted his chin at the crew member in the cabin, still laid-out on the bunk. 'And drag Boof outta there.'

'Yes boss.'

Standing aside to let them pass, the man with the silver buckle stared down at Modeen, who was beginning to regain control of her body. Bending, he held the Taser in front of her face, its two thin wires still connected to the electrodes embedded in her abdomen. 'You behave yourself,' he growled, 'or I'll jam my finger on this sucker and keep it there.'

Modeen gave a tiny nod of acknowledgement. Her whole body felt heavy and drained of energy. The last thing she wanted was another jolt from that *damn* Taser.

After dragging their groggy colleague out of the cabin, the two crew members helped her to her feet and marched her back inside, plonking her down on the bunk. With the Taser's leads still connected to Modeen, the man with the silver buckle followed her inside, unclipping the cartridge from the front of the Taser and letting it drop to the floor. Taking a new cartridge out of a pocket, he fitted it into the Taser and then took a seat on the bunk opposite her, watching as the two crewmen finished securing her to the bulkhead.

'Good.' He jerked his head toward the open doorway. 'Now get out.'

They left without speaking, but Modeen's eyes were fixed on the man with the silver buckle. A tiny groan escaped her lips as she sat up straighter to face him.

Glancing down, she followed the wires from the two electrodes to the spent cartridge on the floor. Her hands were less than steady when she yanked the electrodes from her stomach, flinging them aside in disgust.

The man eyed her with cocky amusement. 'As you see, we can do this the easy way, or the hard way.' He grinned, his teeth white against his dark skin. 'We've been ordered to deliver you unharmed and in one piece, and that's what we intend to do. However, if you cause us any more trouble you *will* get hurt.'

In the face of her level, impassive stare, he said jauntily, 'I think I've made my point.' Rising, he waved the Taser at the porridge dripping from the bulkhead. 'I'll leave you to enjoy your breakfast.' He went to the doorway, where he paused. 'And for your sake, I hope we don't have a repeat performance at lunch time.'

Feeling the gradual return of her strength and composure, Modeen cleared her throat and croaked, 'Ordered by who? And where are you taking me?'

The man narrowed his eyes at her. 'You're going to be on this boat for a week, so I'd advise you to sit back and enjoy the ride.' When the door swung closed behind him, dimness returned to the cabin.

At the sound of the key being turned firmly in the lock, Modeen exhaled, lowered her forearms to her knees, and cupped her face in her hands.

CHAPTER ELEVEN

Wolf's expression darkened. Scowling and gritting his teeth, he swallowed his vexation at being strapped in to what was basically a giant baby walker, and forced his legs to move. The walking aid's under-torso supports and rigid frame on castors supported his weight and held him upright as he made his cumbersome way to the end of the corridor. After executing a clumsy turn, he began making his way back again.

The watching physiotherapist called, 'That's enough for this morning, Troy. You're progressing well – better than well, in fact – but we don't want to overdo it.'

'Just one more lap,' Wolf ground out, his face working. A bead of sweat slid from his temple down his cheek and dropped off his stubbled chin.

The young physio pushed himself off the wall and

made to move toward him. 'No more. You've done enough already.'

Wolf took another tortuous step and growled through clenched teeth, *'I'll* say when I've had enough—'

'You heard the man, soldier.' Ben strode up to give Wolf's shoulder a friendly thump. 'I wasn't expecting to see you out of bed so soon, mate. Considering you were in a coma for over three weeks, you're making great progress.' He stepped aside as Wolf awkwardly manoeuvred back to his room, adding, 'Even the doctor says so.'

Embarrassed at having been seen in the walker by someone other than medical staff – and his CO to boot – Wolf grudgingly submitted to being assisted out of the hated contraption by the physio and a hovering orderly, who then helped him back into bed. He remained sitting upright and nodded to the orderly, who raised the top portion of the hospital bed to a forty-five degree angle and then handed him a pair of dumbbells from the bedside table. Taking one in each hand, Wolf settled himself and began raising them alternately.

The watching physio gave a bemused shake of his head. Lifting an eyebrow at Ben the young man muttered, 'He's done double his assigned walking and now he's doing preacher curls … the guy's a machine.'

Ben grinned. 'Oh, you don't know the half of it. He was one of the fittest – and toughest – soldiers in the Special Forces, which is probably the reason he's recovering so quickly.'

'Ah … he was in the military.' The physio nodded.

'That explains his underlying physique … and attitude.' He threw Ben a wry grin and then, indicating for the orderly to accompany him, left the room.

Ben pulled a chair to the bedside and sat silently watching his friend strain and grunt as he forced his upper body to comply. When he paused to rest, blowing hard, Ben said quietly, 'I can see you're improving physically, mate, but what about your memories? Anything coming back to you?'

Wolf frowned and wiped the sweat from his face with a brawny but unsteady arm, muttering, 'Not much to report on that, sir.'

'We're not in the military now, mate,' Ben said evenly, 'so call me Ben.'

Wolf nodded and went on in a lighter tone. 'I did find out one thing, though. Apparently I'm into Matthew Reilly books,' and he tilted his head at the novel on the bedside table. 'Judging by the bookmark I was already halfway through that one, and found another in the drawer as well.'

'Oh yeah? And do you remember what they were about?'

Wolf shook his head. 'Nah.' He resumed his bicep curl repetitions. a thoughtful frown creasing his brow. 'Although the words were kinda familiar in places. Anyway,' he puffed, 'I ended up starting that one from the beginning … think I'm pretty much back to where the bookmark was.'

'You enjoying it?'

'It's not a bad read. I like the fast pace.' Wolf paused and lowered the dumbbells to look Ben in the eye. 'Jake said Jo was readin' to me while I was out of it … in the coma.'

Ben gazed back at him levelly. 'That's right. She spent a fair bit of time by your side.'

Reaching up a hand, Wolf fingered the ring on the chain around his neck, making the diamonds glint under the overhead lights. 'I guessed as much. The nurses keep askin' me where she is, and … I was wondering if she has anything to do with this?' He held out the ring so Ben could see it. When this garnered no comment, Wolf brought the ring closer to his face again and stared at it, turning it over in his fingers. 'One thing's for sure, it's not a man's ring … don't think it'd get past the first knuckle on my little finger. But if I'd given it to someone why is it here with me?'

He let the ring fall back onto his chest and looked enquiringly at Ben, who remained tight-lipped. Frowning, Wolf muttered, 'I can only assume it didn't go well otherwise the woman I gave it to would be wearing it … *and* she'd be here with me now.'

'Wolf….' Ben exhaled and lowered his gaze to the floor. 'Look, it's … complicated.'

'Complicated?' Wolf's frown darkened. 'Then maybe I should be talkin' to her, so she can *uncomplicate* it for me.'

'That would be my recommendation, only….' Ben

swallowed and raised his head. 'She's dropped off the radar. We don't know where she is.'

'She works for you too?'

Ben hesitated a second, and then nodded.

'Is she on a mission?'

'You could say that.' Ben's lips tightened.

Wolf gave a frustrated huff. 'Don't tell me … it's classified, right?'

Ben met his eyes but said nothing.

Wolf sat back with a grunt. 'You didn't deny that she's got something to do with this,' and he tapped the ring on his chest, 'so can you at least tell me what she's like, this Jo?'

Taking his mobile from a pocket, Ben tapped on the screen and then held it out for Wolf to see the image of five dusty soldiers in full battle dress smiling into the camera.

'Our unit, in Afghanistan,' Ben announced. 'Me, you, JD, Bugs and Spooky. JD's front and centre.'

Wolf took the phone from him and studied the picture. He zoomed in to examine each face carefully before moving on to the next. He lingered longest over Modeen, saying enquiringly, 'JD?'

'That's what I call her.' Ben gave a small smile. 'Josephine Dakota Modeen … JD. Most other people call her Modeen.'

Dragging his eyes away from her dust-smeared, smiling face beneath an equally dusty combat helmet, Wolf murmured drily, 'Well, I recognise myself, and you.'

Holding the phone toward Ben, he pointed to Spooky's grinning face and said pensively, 'And I think that's Luke Jackson. But as for the other two, or when and where the photo was taken….' He scowled and shook his head. 'Nothin'.'

Taking back his phone, Ben said evenly, 'Don't worry, your memories will come back to you in due course, like your physical fitness is already doing. You should be thankful you didn't lose all of them, just the more recent ones.'

'Yeah,' Wolf muttered bitterly, 'at least I recalled my own name so I'm one up on Jason Bourne.'

Ben gave an amused snort. 'Just concentrate on your recovery for now, and try not to overdo it.'

'Not overdo it? The wolfman? As if!' The two men glanced over to see Spooky stroll into the room, grinning. His hair was slicked back and he was dressed in a stylish brown leather bomber jacket over a black skivvy tucked into blue jeans. 'Hey, mate,' he said cheerily, extending Wolf a hand, 'good to see ya finally awake.'

Wolf gazed at him while shaking his hand. 'Luke?'

Spooky clapped him on the shoulder. 'That's right, big fella.'

When Ben's mobile buzzed and vibrated, he glanced at the screen and rose to his feet. Indicating that he'd take the call outside he headed toward the door, throwing Spooky an approving nod as he left.

. . .

'Hey Ben, James here.'

'What've you found?'

'The transit van left the M1 at Pimpama, north of Hope Island on the Gold Coast, but that's as far as I could follow it with the traffic cameras.'

Sensing eagerness in James' voice Ben prompted, 'And?'

'And I ran the van's licence plate. Turns out it was hired from a Brisbane company that has GPS trackers fitted to all their vehicles,' James announced smugly. 'I'll text you a Google Earth map of the route the van took. After I played the national security trump card, the hire company's manager was most obliging and even volunteered information. According to his records, the van was hired two days ago by one Gerard Wallen and returned to the depot yesterday. The manager tracked down the staff member who served Wallen and asked for a description. The staffer was a bit vague, but did tell his boss that Wallen was a big bloke with a Kiwi accent and looked to be of Maori descent.'

'Excellent work, James.' As Ben ended the call his phone pinged with an incoming text. He opened the message and clicked on the attached image file, to see a blue line snaking from the M1 motorway at Pimpama following Jacob Wells Road toward Woongoolba, and dead-ending just before a jetty at the end of Steiglitz Road.

Ben zoomed in on the jetty and saw what looked like a large industrial shed positioned on the northern side.

They must've back-tracked to the M1 along the same route, which means they've either offloaded their 'cargo' to that shed or onto a boat.

Ben narrowed his eyes and pressed his lips together.

Or worse, a sea plane.

'Well it's no wonder you don't remember Bugs or Modeen,' Spooky said, 'we only met them when we signed up for the SASR, which was after your stint in the Regulars.'

'Yeah, that's what Ben said. But the last thing I remember is *being* in the Regulars.'

'The rest'll come back to you, mate, just give it time.'

'Ben said that too.' Wolf shook his head and exhaled. Neither spoke for a moment and then Wolf said thoughtfully, 'You know, I recall seeing female soldiers in Afghanistan, but I didn't think any women had made it into the Special Forces.'

'Modeen was the first.' There was a hint of pride in Spooky's voice. Seeing Wolf's raised eyebrow, he added, 'She's as tough as they come, not to mention clever. And she saved our butts plenty of times.' When Wolf didn't say anything Spooky frowned at him. 'You really don't remember anything about her?'

'Nah, nothing.' Wolf scowled. 'And it's startin' to bug me.'

With a teasing, 'You poor bastard,' Spooky thumped him on the shoulder. ''Cos she's something of a looker, not to mention a formidable force. And more than capable of kicking your ass if you don't remember her, so I'd be searching that memory if I were you.' Chuckling, he was about to show Wolf some photos on his mobile when Ben came back into the room.

He barked, 'Need you on the Gold Coast, Spook, ASAP,' and then glanced at Wolf. 'I'll see you again soon, mate.'

Throwing Ben a brisk nod, Spooky rose from the chair. 'Nice chatting with you, Wolfman.' He extended a fist for Wolf to bump and said cheerily, 'Next time,' before following Ben from the room.

Wolf lowered his arm and listened to their footsteps grow more distant as they strode purposefully down the corridor and away. Catching the sound of a single tread coming toward his room he looked up, thinking Ben might've returned, only to see his bother Jake in the doorway. Drawling, 'Stagger me! It's like Grand Central Station around here,' Wolf gave an amused snort.

Jake came in, grinning. 'Nice to see you too, bro.'

'Yeah, well you'll get a friendlier greeting when you've come to take me outta this place.'

Jake raised a bemused eyebrow and bent to rest his hands on the back of the chair Spooky had just vacated. 'I've spoken to the doctor. He's pretty amazed at the pace of your recovery. Said your respiratory and circulatory systems are in excellent condition, and the latest CAT scan of your noggin is all clear. So it's all good news.' He leaned in to give Wolf a brotherly thump on the arm.

'They're gonna remove your catheter today, and once they're happy with your motor skills, you could be outta here in a coupl'a days.'

With an exuberant, 'Yes!' Wolf punched the air above his head.

'But you'll need a walking frame or crutches for a while,' Jake cautioned. 'Amber's setting up the spare room for you back at the farm as we speak.'

'Amber?'

'You know, my wife?'

'If you say so.'

Smiling lopsidedly, Jake shook his head at his brother. 'You sounded just like Mum then.'

'Oh yeah?' Wolf chuckled. 'How's she travellin', anyhow? Would've expected to see her before this, she was always hangin' out to see me the instant I came home on leave.'

Jake's grin dissolved. 'You don't remember?'

'Remember what?'

The two brothers stared at each other and then Jake sighed and lowered his gaze to the floor. Scuffing the tiles with the toe of his boot, he murmured, 'We … um … had to put her into care … dementia.'

'Oh.' Wolf's face fell. 'Crap.'

'You said it.'

———

By midday the ocean breeze had picked up, creating white caps all around the *North Island Star*. As her bow fronted the mounting swell, rising to crest a wave one moment and then falling into a trough the next, thumps and rattles resounded throughout her structure.

Sitting on her bunk, her back against the bulkhead, Modeen noted the increasing roll and wondered where she was … and where she was going. As the cabin door swung open and brilliant rays of midday sun beamed through the opening like a spotlight, she shaded her eyes against the sudden glare.

An instant later the light was partially blocked as a tentative Boof stepped over the ridge at the base of the door to deposit her lunch offering on the table at the front of the bulkhead. Keeping his dark eyes fixed on her the whole time, he cautiously backed out again, leaving the door ajar to allow fresh air and light to filter into the room.

She waited until her eyes had adjusted before sitting forward to inspect the offerings. Beside a paper cup of water, a plate with what looked like braised steak on a bed of lumpy mashed potato had a plastic fork jammed into its centre like a flimsy flag pole. She gave a disdainful sniff.

Straight out of a can no doubt.

She shrugged.

Then again, that might be a good thing. Fishing trawlers aren't renowned for having outstanding hygiene.

When she reached for the plate, she felt the weight of the handcuffs and chain on her left wrist.

Good thing I'm a righty.

She shook her wrist, knowing these bonds would prove more of a challenge to remove than the ropes she'd broken out of earlier. But right now her muscles were recovering from the shock of the Taser hit, the pain of which was still fresh in her mind. And hunger made her feel more compliant.

For now....

———

In his NatSec Aurion, Bugs peered across the bonnet at the storage facility. He raised the compact 10x42 Steiner Tactical binoculars to his eyes and once more checked the compound for movement. At a vibrating buzz from the centre console, he put down the binoculars and picked up his phone.

'Peterson.'

'Sit-rep, Bugs.'

'Yeah, Ben. I have Green Hills Storage under surveillance. Nothin' much to report, but say the word and I'll kick down the door.'

'Change of plans, Bugs. I need you to catch the next flight to Brisbane, rendezvous with Spook, and then the two of you are to head to the Gold Coast. We have new intel on JD's whereabouts.'

Even before Ben finished speaking Bugs had fired up

the Aurion's V6 engine. 'On my way.' He spun the car around with a squeal of tyres as Ben went on.

'Spooky has the details and is en route. I've organised a vehicle for him in Brisbane and he'll pick you up from the airport. And Bugs?'

'Yeah?'

'Use extreme caution. If that's where they're holding her, there's no telling how many hostiles you'll encounter. And they've managed to capture JD, so we're not dealing with amateurs.'

With an abrupt, 'Noted,' Bugs ended the call and sped away.

CHAPTER TWELVE

Stepping off the Virgin Blue Airbus at Brisbane Airport, Bugs headed to the baggage collection area and stood beside the carousel displaying his flight number. While waiting for his duffel to appear through the rubber curtains, he pulled out his mobile and sent a quick text message, keeping an eye on the now slowly moving baggage carousel. When his bag appeared he bent and collected it in one smooth movement, lifting it onto a broad shoulder before making his way through the crowd and striding to the exit.

Outside the terminal building, he strolled past the queues of commuters waiting for taxis and then stopped at the passenger pick-up point. Dropping his duffel at his feet he stretched, squinting in the glare of the early afternoon Queensland sun.

A short distance along the terminal to his right, a black Toyota Aurion snaked its way past slower moving vehicles and then rolled to a stop in front of him. Its darkly tinted windows made it difficult to see inside, but when the driver revved the motor as though impatient, Bugs grinned. Grabbing his duffel he opened the door and jumped into the front passenger's side. He had just enough time to fist-bump the driver before being thrown back in his seat as the vehicle pulled away from the curb with an aggressive motor roar and squeal of tyres.

With a cheery, 'What time did ya get in, Spook?' he threaded his bag between the two front seats and tossed it into the back.

''Bout an hour ago, but I only just got back from NatSec's storage facility in Eagle Farm. Ben arranged for me to pick up the car from there. He wants us heavy.'

Bugs gave a small nod, having already assumed as much. 'Where's she being held?'

'Hopefully here.' Tapping on his phone, Spooky handed it to Bugs. 'A large boat shed at a jetty between here and the Gold Coast. I've punched the address into the GPS.'

Bugs zoomed in on the screen image. 'So ... he doesn't know for *sure* she's there?'

'Nah, but it's our best lead so far.'

Peering closely at the image Bugs muttered, 'If she is there here's hopin' we make it in time. 'Cos if they've put her on a boat there's no tellin' where they've taken her.'

Flicking the indicator, Spooky took the Moreton Drive ramp south onto the Gateway Motorway and accelerated to highway speed. He jerked a thumb at the glove box and lifted his chin at Bugs. 'By the way, I brought you a present.'

Throwing him a questioning grin, Bugs leaned forward to open the glove box. His eyes widened when he took out a point fifty calibre Desert Eagle and two spare clips. Stroking the weapon, he crooned, 'Aww....' before throwing Spooky a wide, toothy grin. 'I love you, man.'

Forty-five minutes later the black Aurion turned east onto Steiglitz Road, a narrow dual carriageway flanked on both sides by tall sugar cane.

Still cradling the Desert Eagle in his lap, Bugs glanced at the GPS and announced, 'Should be comin' up about two hundred metres on our left,' while loading a round into the pistol. 'What's our plan of attack, Spook?' He clicked the safety on as the vehicle rolled to a stop on the verge beside the cane field.

Holding his mobile so they could both see it, Spooky zoomed in on the shed near the jetty. 'This is our target, the shed on the corner of Kleinschmidt and Steiglitz roads.'

Bugs gave an amused huff. 'With those names I wouldn't be surprised if we were takin' on the Nazis 'stead of the Kiwis.'

Throwing him a wry grin, Spooky continued. 'Looks like the shed's joined to the one alongside it, and there's a coupl'a other buildings in the same compound.' He moved the image down. 'There's a carpark and boat ramp beyond the buildings. I suggest we do a casual drive-by, chuck a left at Kleinschmidt, and cruise around to the boat ramp.'

At Bugs' frowned, 'This vehicle isn't your everyday suburban sedan or boat-towing ute so we might attract attention … what if they open up on us?' Spooky shrugged. 'Guess we take that as confirmation we're in the right place. Besides, we'll be OK.' He tapped on the windscreen. 'This baby's got body armour and bullet-proof windows.'

'Sounds good to me.' Bugs rubbed his large, freckled hands together. 'And I always prefer a stand-up fight to sneakin' around.'

Leaning down to press the boot release, Spooky checked the side and rear view mirrors before opening the driver's door and throwing Bugs a nod. 'Let's load up.'

At the boot, as they locked and loaded two MP5SD6s, Bugs enquired hopefully, 'What about the Vanquish?'

Without looking at him Spooky replied, 'Throw it in the back. That way it'll be within reach if we need it.'

After laying the weapons on the back seat, the men resumed their places in the front and Spooky started the Aurion. As the vehicle cruised along the road Bugs murmured, 'Just two blokes takin' a leisurely drive,' while keeping his eyes peeled for any sudden or unusual activity.

After slowing the car to a crawl, Spooky turned left into Kleinschmidt Road before the boat shed and then circled around the back of the compound to the boat ramp. After a quick perusal he muttered, 'The place looks dead.'

Peering out of his window while still projecting a casual air, Bugs drawled, 'There's nothin' much happenin' here either. The carpark's deserted save for a coupl'a four-by-fours with empty boat trailers.' He glanced at Spooky. 'Let's head back to the jetty.'

Nodding, Spooky reversed the Aurion. As they passed the eastern side of the boat shed he turned to idle along Steiglitz Road again. In front of them an old bloke in soapsuds-grey baggy shorts and a paint-splattered light blue tee shirt was sliding the boat yard's gate closed.

'Pull up here.' Bugs buzzed down the window to call, 'Oi, buddy,' at the bloke on the gate.

The man flicked them an irritated glance and shouted, 'We close at four.'

Bugs nodded his understanding but persisted. 'What's the story with the jetty?' He pointed over the bonnet to the locked gate at the end of the road.

The man stopped what he was doing and sauntered over to the car. As he approached, Spooky leaned behind to throw his jacket over the weaponry on the back seat.

'It's a private jetty,' the man mumbled through gappy teeth, ''n ya have'ta be paid-up in advance to berth there.' He pointed a grubby finger. 'The office's just around the back past the boat ramp.'

As though enquiring about the weather, Bugs said evenly, 'Why the heavy security?'

The man sneered, 'It ain't heavy enough.' He leaned an arm on the Aurion's roof, and Bugs had to swallow a grimace at the sour body odour that assaulted his nostrils. 'Some arsehole broke in just the other night.' The man licked his cracked lips. 'Luckily nothin' was stolen. But we're thinkin' of puttin' in cameras.'

In a slightly strangled voice Bugs said, 'Sounds like a good idea.' Signalling with a tilt of his head for Spooky to get going, he added, 'Anyway, thanks mate,' and buzzed up his window. As soon as they were out of earshot he turned to Spooky with a shake of his head. 'Man that guy stinks.' Pulling a face and muttering, 'Week-old fish guts, bad breath and BO,' he turned the fan on the air conditioning panel to maximum and focused the nearest vents on himself.

Chuckling and buzzing down his own window, Spooky nosed the car to a stop in front of the gates to the jetty. 'Reckon old stinky was telling the truth?'

Bugs kept his face in the flow of air from the vents when he answered, 'Except for the killer pong he wasn't armed and seemed pretty genuine. Didn't look like a crim to me. But I reckon we should ask a few questions at the office while we're waiting for him to finish lockin' up and nick off for the day. Then we'll take a look inside the shed.'

'Right-o. I'll check out the office while you call Ben with an update. I reckon he'll be hanging out to hear from us.'

'No doubt, but what do I tell him? There's nothin' much to report.'

Spooky sighed. 'Yeah, whatever's happened here, I think we missed it.'

————

Heaving himself onto the parallel walking bars with a grunt, Wolf locked his arms and eased his body weight onto his legs. Holding onto the bars for stability, he took his first tentative step, his face a picture of determination.

The watching physiotherapist said mildly, 'I don't suppose there's much point in telling you not to overdo this?'

Ignoring him, Wolf gritted his teeth and shuffled his arms forward, willing his legs to follow. His whole body juddered as he transferred his weight onto his left leg and dragged up his right foot. Once it was steady and able to take his weight, he shuffled his arms again and did the same with his left foot.

An hour later he'd made good progress, earning himself a pat on the back from the physio. This time, when told he'd done enough and instructed to return to his room, an exhausted Wolf complied without argument.

————

Taking them two at a time, Spooky bounded down the office steps and jogged to the waiting Aurion. He jumped into the driver's seat as Bugs put down his mobile and glanced at him.

'Ben's of the same opinion as us. If she were here, there'd be guards or some other tell-tale sign.'

Spooky exhaled and settled back in his seat. 'So, what next?'

'He still wants us to check the compound, to be sure.'

'Right-o.' Spooky was about to start the car's engine when Bugs' next words gave him pause.

'And there's something else.'

'Yeah?' Lowering his hand from the ignition, Spooky eyed Bugs. 'What?'

'Apparently Salty found something of interest in Modeen's apartment.'

'Salty?' Spooky frowned. 'What the frig has Salty got to do with this?'

Bugs gave a throaty laugh. 'Don't underestimate "The Saltman". He's got fingers in lots of pies.'

'Yeah, he's a good bloke. I didn't mean any insult, just wondered how and why he got involved in this.' At Bugs' 'who knows' shrug in response, Spooky went on. 'So what did he find?'

'A list that Ben suspects Modeen may've obtained when she went after Reger.'

'A list of *what?*'

Hearing the impatience in his friend's voice, Bugs chortled, 'OK, keep your shirt on. It's a list of names of ten Black Mamba members. Reger's on it. Ben suspects Modeen's been workin' her way through it, which is probably why she's gone missing.'

When Spooky murmured, 'Working her way through it?' Bugs raised an eyebrow at him.

'Ben didn't elaborate, but some of the names have been crossed out, so it doesn't take a genius to figure what was goin' on.'

'So she's been kickin' arse 'n takin' names?' Spooky shook his head. 'Well … crap! Why didn't she let us in on that action?'

'Hey, if I knew what goes on inside females' minds I wouldn't be divorced,' Bugs said drily. 'But if I had to hazard a guess, I'd say the whole Wolf thing really got to her.'

Spooky nodded and both men were silent for a long moment. Then he said, 'How many names are left on the list?'

'Ben didn't say.'

Starting the engine, Spooky put the car into drive. As they accelerated away, Bugs said, 'Did you get anything from the office?'

'Not much, just the names and registrations of the boats berthed here, all commercial fishing rigs. They've been out working and aren't expected back 'til next week. The office also confirmed old stinky's story about the break-in at the jetty.' Spooky gave an amused snort. 'The lady on the desk thought I was the guy come to give them a quote on installing security cameras.'

'That a sideline ya haven't told me about?' Bugs teased.

'I wish!'

Bugs shook his head, still grinning. 'Nah, you'd be bored out of your brain.'

'You're probably right.'

'So where're we headin' now?'

'To the roadhouse off the main drag. We'll come back here after dark to finish our sweep.'

'Right, what's going on?' NatSec regional operations manager Jack Pender strode into the office to stand in front of the desk, arms folded across his chest, staring down at Ben.

Keeping his expression carefully neutral, Ben looked up to say pleasantly, 'G'day Jack.'

Jack's eyes narrowed. 'You know better than to try that look on me, Ben.'

'What look?'

'Humph!' Jack lifted one reproachful eyebrow. 'Surely you didn't think the fact you've re-deployed two of our assets – who, by the way, had already been assigned other missions – wouldn't come to my attention?'

Ben sat back and returned his level gaze. 'I had every intention of keeping you in the loop, Jack. I only delayed informing you because I wanted to gather more intel on a troubling issue that's arisen.'

With a grunt, Jack unfolded his arms and settled himself in a chair.

Watching him, Ben went on. 'Besides, I replaced them with two other agents.'

'That's not the point but go on, I'm listening.'

'One of our operatives has dropped off the radar, we assume abducted … possibly neutralised.'

Jack frowned and said gruffly, 'I believe I saw paperwork for the operative in question which indicated she'd resigned from NatSec. So if she's chosen to pursue a civilian life, why are you assuming Ms Bennet has met with some misadventure?' He threw Ben a significant glance. 'And why would her movements still be our concern?'

'Because I believe her disappearance is linked to event 0742.'

'The Reger event?'

Ben nodded. 'And as such, the situation could pose a security risk.' In the face of Jack's wordless, assessing gaze he added, 'And then there's the organisation's duty of care to our employees, past and present.'

'Hmm … as far as justifications go, Ben, this is a tad flimsy. But I see where you're coming from.' Jack eyed him thoughtfully for a long moment. 'Speaking of our duty of care, how is Troy Ryan's recovery going?'

Ben's expression lifted a fraction. 'He's out of the coma and doing well apart from a few memory gaps, which the doctors indicate should be temporary.'

Nodding slowly, Jack rubbed his chin. 'And now

Josephine has gone missing under suspicious circumstances.'

'That's correct.'

'And you have some idea who's behind it?'

'Because of their link to that event, I believe the "Black Mambas" are more than likely responsible.'

Jack continued nodding. 'Well ... considering Josephine's activities since the Julia Creek operation, I can understand why the Mambas would want her out of the way.'

Ben sat forward and eyed him intently. 'So, do I have your permission to escalate this event?'

'What are we talking about here?' Jack met his gaze. 'Specifically, what resources do you need?'

'Williams and Peterson for another week, max. And some satellite time.'

'Why Williams and Peterson in particular?'

'As you know, we were part of a tight-knit unit in the Special Forces and I need every advantage in this situation.'

Jack cupped his hands over his nose and mouth, pressing his fingers against the bridge of his nose and gazing at Ben over them. Then, taking a deep breath, he lowered his arms and rocked back in the chair. 'Approved. One point of note....' He paused before going on. 'If one Nakahi Pango were neutralised during your efforts, the powers-that-be would not be disappointed.'

Turning to his laptop, Ben was about to put fingers to

keyboard when Jack barked, 'Don't bother, Nakahi's not on the list.' When Ben raised his eyebrows, Jack gave a snort and shook his head, a grin twitching the corners of his mouth. 'You also didn't think I knew about the list?' He clicked his tongue in mock reproach. 'We're an intelligence agency, remember? As operations manager, it's my job to know what's going on … and I expect to be kept up to date by my team leaders.'

Ben's brow creased. 'So … Nakahi Pango?'

'Loosely translated it means "Black Serpent".'

'So….'

'Yes.' Jack nodded. 'Also known as "The Black Mamba".'

Turning to his laptop again, Ben opened a file on the memory stick and scrolled down until he found a jpeg image. He enlarged it and spun the laptop so Jack could see the screen capture Modeen had taken from Reger's computer, when she'd confronted him in the middle of an online chat session in his Bunbury motel room.

Confronted him … and then neutralised him.

Jack sat forward to study the image, taking in the tribal tattoos covering one side of the man's dark-skinned, square-jawed face framed by whiskery grey dreadlocks. His blackened lips were open, revealing the equally black-stained interior of his mouth. Above it, cold blue eyes completed the menacing image.

Jack muttered, 'His real name is Owen Patel. And don't bother checking the list, that name's not on there either. We confirmed his ID by other means.'

'What else do we have on him?'

'I'll make the file available to you, but this is all …,' and Jack raised his eyes to stare into Ben's, '… off the record.'

Ben nodded. 'Understood. And thanks, Jack.'

Rising, Jack headed to the door and then stopped to look back at Ben. 'If you get her back alive, will that be an end to this matter?'

Ben took his time replying. 'Hard to say.' He ran a hand over his face. 'I believe a lot depends on Ryan's recovery. I can only say one thing for sure … if she's still alive, her captors are the ones in danger.'

Nodding, Jack murmured sombrely, 'Well, let's hope it *will* be over. In this instance I'm prepared to look the other way … but we can't have one of our agents going rogue.' With that he strode out, just as the phone on Ben's desk buzzed.

Still frowning, Ben checked the caller ID and pressed Answer. 'Bugs,' he barked, 'sit rep.'

'We've had a look around and this place is clean, Ben. Spook had a chat to the office staff. They confirmed there've been boats comin' and goin' as you'd expect, but they reckon they've never had a seaplane berth at the jetty. They also said a seaplane landing in the vicinity, day or night, would attract attention, and I reckon they're right about that. So our best guess is that she's been taken away by boat.'

'Roger that, Bugs. You two head back to Brisbane.

I've managed to escalate the event at this end and might have more intel for you in the morning.'

'What about Cecil Hills?'

'It's on the back-burner for the moment. Right now we need to focus on finding JD.'

———

At his doctor's cheery greeting of, 'How are we this morning?' Wolf replied sourly, 'I don't know how *you* are, but I'm still in *here*,' and he jutted his chin to indicate the hospital room.

Checking the chart at the foot of the bed, the doctor murmured with an air of amused tolerance, 'So I see.'

Wolf glowered at him and was about to snarl a response when the doctor raised a hand and said crisply, 'I've been talking with your physiotherapist, and to the relief of all the ward staff,' and he flicked Wolf a wry glance, 'we're happy to advise that, provided you have the support you need at home, you're ready to be discharged.'

Ignoring the jibe, Wolf sat up in bed and said sharply, 'I can get outta here ... today?'

'Yes, as long as we can organise a wheelchair and crutches for you, and regular home physiotherapy sessions.'

Even before the doctor finished his brief visit, a grinning Wolf was dialling a number on his mobile. When

Jake answered his call, Wolf drawled, 'Hey bro. You comin' in this morning?'

'Plannin' to be in just after lunch, why?'

'Doc says I can go home.'

This met with silence and then Jake said carefully, 'That's great … but what about your physiotherapy, don't you need to continue with that? And how will we get you out of the hospital and into the car?'

'The doc's organising physio house calls, or some such thing,' Wolf rapped, sounding impatient, 'and a wheelchair and crutches.'

'Why the rush, Troy? Are you sure you don't want to leave it for another day or two? The hospital has the equipment and expertise on hand, everything you need to hasten your recovery.'

Wolf's expression darkened and he growled, 'Jake, I feel like I'm missin' a big part of my life, and this place is draggin' me down. It's so sterile, and the staff are so *determined* to be cheerful. It's depressing. I need to get out and breathe the fresh air. I'm on the mend and won't be any trouble, if that's what you and what's-her-name are worried about.'

'If you mean my wife, her name's Amber. You might want to remember that.'

'Yeah, yeah. So, you comin' to get me or what? You did say you had a room ready for me at the farm, right?'

'Yeah, we do.' Jake's resigned sigh reverberated down the phone line. 'OK Troy, it's your call.'

'Thanks, bro. So I'll see you soon?'

Jake sighed again. 'I'll be there this afternoon.'

In the mission briefing room at NatSec's Melbourne headquarters, Ben looked up when IT guru James entered. Without bothering with preliminaries, he said crisply, 'Do seafaring vessels have transponders? Can we track them the same way we do aircraft?'

Unperturbed by the abrupt questioning, James nodded and strode to Ben's side. 'Every ship over a certain tonnage is required by law to be fitted with an AIS, an automatic identification system.' Leaning in, he clicked on the search window of Ben's web browser and entered the search string 'marine traffic'. He selected the first link that came up in the list and a map of the world opened on screen. When he plugged a USB cable into the laptop, the image was transmitted to a huge heads-up display covering the wall of the briefing room.

Taking control of his laptop again, Ben zoomed in on Australia and then on the Queensland Gold Coast. When a mass of red, green, yellow, blue, and orange triangles appeared on screen, he glanced at James. 'These represent maritime vessels, right?'

James nodded.

'And this is in real time?'

'Yep.'

'Can I go back in time? I want to see any vessels that entered Tipplers Passage up to two days ago.'

'Yeah, but you need to log-in to access all the program's functionality.' Leaning in again, James brought up a sign-in screen and typed in a NatSec user ID and password. He clicked on the time lapse drop-down menu and selected twelve hours prior. When the screen repopulated, he waved the mouse so the cursor looped over one location. 'See this slide bar? You can use it to transition back and forward in time.'

Ben took control of the mouse again and moved the slide bar down, watching as the coloured triangles relocated about the screen. 'Way too many to follow,' he muttered, frowning. 'How do you filter the types of vessels displayed?'

'What are you looking for?'

'Don't know exactly, but I'm pretty certain it wouldn't be a passenger liner, a tanker, or a large cargo ship. If I were to hazard a guess, I'd say it's more likely to be a commercial fishing vessel.'

'Like a trawler?' At Ben's nod James took the mouse from him once more. Clicking on another drop-down menu, he made some changes to the program's settings. The wall display repopulated, this time without the dark blue, yellow, red and most of the green triangles. 'Now we're only seeing small cargo, fishing, and recreational vessels.'

'Much better.' Ben took over again and worked the time lapse slide bar, watching a few of the remaining triangles moving in and out of Tipplers Passage.

Not one of them went anywhere near the jetty at the end of Steiglitz Road.'

He panned out to get a wider view of the area and adjusted the time lapse again.

'Hey, look there.' James pointed at the wall-mounted screen.

'What?'

'An orange triangle just disappeared off the map, here,' and he pointed to a spot in the ocean off the west coast of New Zealand.

Ben toggled the slide back and the triangle returned to view, only to disappear again when he moved the slide forward. 'How can that be?'

'I'm not sure.' James rubbed his chin. 'Maybe an electrical fault on the ship … or they might've turned off their AIS for some reason. Worse case scenario, maybe the boat sank.'

Ben right-clicked on the triangle and an information window popped up.

Fishing – steel prawn trawler, North Island Star, *Auckland.*

At Ben's triumphant grunt, James frowned. 'Am I missing something? 'Cos to me, this only confirms that a trawler left Auckland about a week ago and then disappeared mid-ocean.'

Sitting back, Ben eyed him with an air of genial satisfaction. 'That's exactly right, James. But for me this also ticks a couple of boxes.'

———

The automatic doors at the front entrance of Royal Hobart Hospital swished open and a wheelchair trundled through, occupied by one large man and pushed from behind by another.

At the feel of the fresh chill of Tasmanian breeze on his skin, Wolf's face broke into a smile and he relaxed in the chair. With a gruff, 'Thanks Jake,' he ran a hand over his closely cropped hair and breathed deeply. 'I'm *so* glad to get out of that place. Feel like now I can finally get my life back.'

Jake thumped him on a broad shoulder. 'You're welcome, mate, but don't try to take things too fast,' at which Wolf merely grunted.

When he stopped on the hospital's wide front concourse, waiting for the traffic to clear so they could cross to the carpark, Jake enquired casually, 'What d'ya think you'll do when you're fully recovered?'

Wolf looked thoughtful. 'I guess that'll be up to Ben. According to him I still have a job,' and he shrugged. 'I have no idea what sort of job, but apparently I didn't suck at it – and there's an apartment waiting for me in Canberra.'

The traffic cleared and Jake jogged across the road, rolling the wheelchair close beside a battered-looking dual-cab four wheel drive. With a curt, 'Wait,' when Wolf made to get out of the chair, he hurried to open the front passenger's door and then helped his impatiently huffing brother into the car. When he went to strap Wolf in, he was met with a surly, 'I can do it, I'm not *completely* useless.'

Sighing, Jake turned his attention to the wheelchair, folding it and packing it into the back of the ute. Climbing into the driver's side, he put the key in the ignition and said with forced cheerfulness, 'Amber's making us some of her special sandwiches to have when we get home,' and started the diesel engine.

'Sounds good to me.' Wolf's tone held a note of apology as though he regretted his previous terseness. 'And I can't wait to see the old farm.'

'Yeah, well apart from a new paddock of grapes, the property's pretty much the same as you'd remember it.' Jake flicked him a glance and then nosed the ute out of the carpark and into the stream of traffic. 'The homestead's a bit different now, though. Amber and I made some alterations after Mum moved out.'

Taking his usual route along Collins Street and onto Barrack, Jake headed toward the intersection linking to the main south-east highway. He slowed as they approached the traffic lights and flicked on the car's right indicator. As the lights changed to green he moved the ute forward, preparing to make the right hand turn, when the insistent horn blast from an approaching Mack truck had him jamming on the brakes and swearing loudly.

Wolf's head jerked forward and then back as the ute squealed to a stop. His eyes widened at the sight of the huge B-double running the red light and making a bee-line for his side of the ute. Leaning as far away as his seatbelt would allow, he closed his eyes and ducked his head while the truck roared past, missing them by millimetres.

After gesturing wildly and shouting obscenities at the fast disappearing semi, Jake looked across at his ashen-faced, visibly shaken brother and put a hand on his shoulder. 'You OK, bro?'

Wolf remained bent over, breathing hard. When Jake shook him gently he gave a curt nod and gulped, 'I'm alright.'

'You sure?' Frowning, Jake put the car into gear and they moved forward. 'You don't look great, you're as white as a sheet. It's not like you to let some half-witted driver scare you so bad. You'd normally be givin' the idiot a mouthful, and some.'

Swearing under his breath, Wolf straightened in his seat and ran a hand over his face. 'I just wasn't expecting to escape the hospital only to have some *freakin'* truck finish me off.' His brow puckered in a perplexed frown. 'And I....'

Seeing his Adam's apple bob in his throat, Jake enquired anxiously, 'And you what?'

'I ... don't know....' Wolf blinked and turned to frown at his brother. 'I saw ... like a vision or something, in slow motion....' His eyes took on a faraway look. 'Of a truck smashin' through a house.' Shaking his head as though to clear it, he went on haltingly, 'It was as if ... I was … there, watchin' it happen.' He paused, grasping at the jumbled sensations and foggy mental images that were already slipping away. 'My gut twisted into knots….' Looking down, he rested a tentative hand on his firm midsection. '… and then … I was running, flat-out.' His head shot up and his voice rose. 'Then this bright light came out of nowhere—'

When he suddenly stopped speaking to stare fixedly ahead, Jake flicked him a worried glance and pulled the ute to the side of the road. With the motor still idling, he turned in his seat to gaze at his brother in concern. 'Maybe I should take you back to the hospital.'

'No!'

'Alright, alright. No need to shout.'

Taking a deep breath, Wolf swallowed and said more calmly, 'Sorry, bro. Look … I'll be fine.' One corner of his lips tipped upward in a teasing grin that didn't meet his eyes. 'Just try to get me home in one piece, will ya?'

After staring at him for a long moment, Jake put the ute in gear and nosed back onto the highway.

CHAPTER FOURTEEN

Lifting the mouldy head of the bunk bed mattress, Modeen slipped her hand beneath it and retrieved the electrode she'd managed to keep from the Tasering she'd received. She stared down at the dart-like electrode and narrowed her eyes. She didn't know when or how, but the man with the silver buckle was going to *pay* for that painful little indignity.

After first cocking her head to listen for any sound of approaching footsteps, she used the electrode to pick open the handcuff attached to her left wrist. Taking care not to let the shackle and heavy chain fall to the floor in case the sound alerted her captors, she gave her hand a shake and rubbed her wrist. Tucking the electrode back under the mattress, she got to her feet and then dropped to the floor to begin a routine of push-ups, sit-ups and squats, all in complete darkness.

Gotta stay fit and ready for anything.

The faint hue of daylight inching its way through the crack beneath her cabin door told her morning was approaching, and she could expect another delivery of porridge from Boof at any moment. By her calculations this would be her third morning on the trawler. Apart from Boof's three visits each day, she had no other contact with the crew and had not been let out of her cell. After their initial, less than friendly encounter, she'd worked at gaining Boof's trust and could tell he was growing more comfortable around her.

Rising to sit on the bunk, she snapped the handcuff on again and leaned her back against the bulkhead to await his arrival.

Her thoughts strayed to Wolf. How was his recovery going? Did he remember what had happened in Julia Creek? Was he wondering why she wasn't there with him? She wondered that herself....

Where was she being taken? It was clear she was wanted alive and unharmed, but for what ... and by who?

The man with the silver buckle had said she'd be on the boat for a week, which by her reckoning would see her halfway around Australia, up to New Guinea, down to Hobart, or across to New Zealand.

New Zealand.

It had been high on her 'places of interest' list, until Wolf's emergence from his coma overshadowed everything else. But now, at the prospect of perhaps meeting the head of the 'Black Mambas', Modeen's eyes narrowed and a vindictive grin tugged at the corner of her mouth.

———

Jake stood at the foot of the bed in the homestead's guest room, frowning at its grim-faced occupant. '*Amber*, my wife's name is Amber.' He thrust both hands on his hips. 'You might be my big brother, Troy, but this is *our* house, Amber's and mine, and you're a guest here.' His frown deepened. 'You remember selling us your half of the property when you joined the Army?'

'That's something I *do* remember.'

'Well, it would also pay you to remember that Amber has a say in whether you stay, or....'

Wolf stared back at him. 'Or what?'

Undeterred by the hardness in his brother's eyes, Jake answered, 'Or I take you back to the hospital.' After giving Wolf a minute to think that over, he said firmly, 'So it's *Amber*, not "Sweet Cheeks", "Blondie" or "The Missus", none of which she appreciates being called.' He sighed. 'Look, she's making an effort to help you feel at home, is it really so hard to at least be courteous to her?'

It was Wolf's turn to sigh. Seeing him bend his head in silent acquiescence, Jake said more calmly, 'So get dressed, breakfast is at eight. You OK to make your way to the dining room on your own?'

'Yeah ... and you're right, I forgot my manners.' Wolf exhaled and rubbed his eyes. 'It's just ... I've been struggling to come to terms with my situation.' Frustration crept into his deep voice. 'And I don't understand why people can't just fill in the gaps for me.'

Jake moved closer and said mildly, 'You can thank the egghead neurologist for that. Something about your neural synaptic pathways needin' to rebuild the connections for themselves ... or some such crock. When I asked him to explain it in layman's terms, the doc said you're better off recalling or working things out for yourself instead of accepting what others tell you, 'specially as everyone has their own take on things. And in any case, I can't really help you with what's happened to you recently. Only your NatSec buddies know what you've been up to the last couple of years, and exactly how you ended up injured. Whenever you visited us you were pretty tight-lipped about what you actually did, even after you left the armed forces.'

'When did I last visit?'

'About eighteen months ago ... and that reminds me.' Jake frowned. 'You offered to "dispose" of Sebastian while you were here, which went over like a lead balloon 'specially with Amber.'

'Who the hell is Sebastian?'

'Amber's ... make that *our* ... Shih Tzu.' At Wolf's blank look, Jake said in a long-suffering tone, 'A dog? A miniature dog. And before you say anything, I'm only too aware it's a waste of space, but it's Amber's fur-baby, so be nice.'

With an unimpressed but otherwise non-committal

grunt Wolf threw back the covers and eased his legs to the edge of the bed. Leaning forward, he clasped the ring dangling from the chain around his neck and held it toward Jake. 'I didn't tell you anything about this?'

Seeing the hope in his brother's eyes, Jake put a hand on his shoulder and gave a small shake of his head. 'But look, Ben implied that you and Josephine were more than just friends, so taking a stab in the dark – and that's all this is. Like I said, you weren't exactly forthcoming with information – I'd suggest you gave the ring to her.'

'To Jo?'

Jake nodded. 'I only met her a few times, but she struck me as someone who was going to stick around.' His brow puckered. 'I'm surprised we haven't seen her since you woke from the coma.'

Wolf stared at him for a long, thoughtful moment and then slipped the ring back beneath his shirt.

———

In the mission briefing room at NatSec HQ, Melbourne, Ben slipped the picture of Owen Patel back into the folder and muttered under his breath, 'AKA Nakahi Pango … AKA The Black Mamba.' Placing the folder on the table in front of him, he tapped on his laptop's keyboard and a map of New Zealand's north island projected onto the heads-up display covering the briefing room's front wall.

He studied the map intently, honing in on the last

known location of Patel, a high-rise building in the middle of Auckland city owned by Rotorua Holdings. When he cross-referenced the *North Island Star* he found it was also owned by Rotorua Holdings, its registered berth in the Wynyard Quarter, Waiheke Island, Auckland. Taking out his mobile, he tapped on one of his contacts, and the Director General of ASIO answered the call on the third ring.

'Bryan, Ben here.'

'Ben Smith! Haven't heard from you for a while. How're things?'

'Good, Bryan. But right now I need some priority surveillance. You able to help out?'

'Sure mate. Just flick me the details in an email and I'll assign it.'

The two men exchanged pleasantries and then Ben ended the call to immediately make another. As soon as he heard it answered he barked, 'Bugs, need you and Spook at Papakura Military Base. Stand by, I'll get Leanne to advise your flight details.'

'Roger, Ben.' Snapping his mobile closed, Bugs turned to Spooky. 'Looks like we're headin' to En-Zed.'

'Which island?'

'North, Papakura.'

'Isn't that where the Kiwi SAS is based?'

'Yep.' Bugs grinned and wiggled his pale eyebrows. 'We might even get a chance to see how the Kiwi Special Forces do things.'

Spooky gave an amused snort. 'I wouldn't count on it if I were you. We're not in the SASR now, remember.'

With an unconcerned shrug, Bugs muttered, 'We'll see. Anyway, Leanne's gonna phone through our flight details so we may as well saddle-up.'

———

Although his legs still felt weak Wolf grit his teeth and left his crutches behind, to shuffle his way to the dining room. As he seated himself at the table opposite Jake, Amber emerged from the kitchen carrying generous servings of bacon and eggs on toast. She put the delicious-smelling plates in front of the two men and then returned to the kitchen, appearing a moment later with a bowl of cereal for herself and one of dog food for Sebastian, her canine shadow. The men waited for her to be seated before tucking in to their breakfast with gusto.

With a hearty burp, Jake set down his knife and fork. 'Pardon me.' He sat back, smiling at his wife as she collected the now empty plates. 'Great brekkie. Thanks, sweetheart.' As he spoke, he threw Wolf a meaningful glance.

'Oh yeah, delicious.' Wolf looked over at his sister-in-law. 'Thanks, Anna.'

Jake bent his head, shaking it in disbelief. Raising it again, he growled, 'Nice try, but her name's *Amber*.'

'It's OK, love.' Amber raised a hand to stop her

husband going any further. 'We've gotta give Troy time to get his memories back.'

Jake merely raised an accusing eyebrow at his brother and sat forward, putting both hands on the table as he prepared to stand. 'I'm headin' down t'the bottom paddock,' he said tightly, 'to pump up some water for the vineyard. Wanna tag along?'

'Sure.' Wolf wobbled a little as he got to his feet. 'Got nothin' better to do.'

'I'll bring the ute around 'n pick you up out the front.'

'Now don't go wearing your brother out. He still needs lots of rest.' Amber rose and headed to the kitchen shadowed by Sebastian, his little pink tongue hanging out and his claws clicking on the floorboards behind her.

Wolf called, 'I'll be OK, thank you … *Amber.*' As he spoke, he flicked Jake a questioning look.

Nodding, Jake mumbled, 'Better,' as he grabbed the keys to his work ute and strode out.

Outside, Wolf raised his eyes to the blue sky and breathed deeply of the fresh country air. Sweeping a glance over the green, undulating landscape, he took in the ghost gums across the valley swaying in the light breeze, and his ears picked up the melodious warble of magpies from the tree tops where wisps of morning mist still clung. He gave an appreciative sigh and then shuffled to the battered four wheel drive ute sitting idling on the gravel path.

From the driver's side Jake sat silently watching as Wolf opened the front passenger door, reversed his butt onto the seat, and then laboriously pulled his legs up and in one at a time. Jake knew better than to try to help, aware his fiercely independent brother would see it as pity and resent the well-meaning gesture. No, he just had to let Troy muddle through himself.

Once Wolf was settled Jake set off toward the bottom of the property. The Wolverton farm was in Huonville, just over forty minutes drive south-west of Hobart. It encompassed a little over a hundred and fifty acres between Rockwood Road and the deeply flowing Huon River, and was surrounded by rolling hills that bordered both sides of the valley.

As the ute bumped down a dirt track Wolf winced and muttered, 'Wanna reverse up for a second, mate?'

'Why?'

'I think you missed a pothole back there.' Wolf threw him a black look. 'Only one, mind you.'

'Very funny.' With a sharp intake of breath, Jake leaned on the brakes bringing the car to a sliding stop. 'Would you look at those cheeky buggers!' He pointed toward the vineyard. 'It's the middle of the morning but that's not stoppin' the rabbits from helpin' themselves to the vines right there, in plain view, bold as freakin' brass.'

Wolf was staring at the furry free-loaders. 'You bring a rifle, bro?'

'I did better than that.' Jake grinned and reached into

the back seat. 'I brought mine *and* yours.' He handed Wolf an old pump action twenty-two before retrieving his own rifle.

Wolf eyed it. 'What've you got there?'

'My new Sportco,' Jake said proudly. 'Bolt action, custom stock, ten round mag and BSA three-to-nine power scope.'

With a droll, 'It's very pretty,' Wolf held out his hand.

'What?' Jake hugged the rifle against his chest as though unwilling to hand it over.

Wolf raised an eyebrow and said drily, 'Ammo?'

'Oh … right.' With a rueful grin, Jake opened the centre console and pulled out a pack of rim fire bullets. Handing three to his brother he said, 'Reckon we'll only get a coupl'a shots off before the buggers bolt.'

Moving slowly, Wolf climbed from the car and leaned against the bonnet to feed the bullets into his rifle's tube magazine.

Jake finished loading his Sportco, mumbling, 'It's gotta be a good eighty to ninety metres, do you want to get closer?'

'Nah, we should be right.' Wolf flashed him a grin. 'After you, little bro.'

Bracing his rifle against the open driver's side door, Jake took aim and let loose one round. Straightening, he swore loudly as all six rabbits leapt with alarm and scampered off. 'Damn it, I missed.'

On the other side of the ute, the barrel of Wolf's twenty-two silently followed the fleeing targets. Then,

Pop! Pump, Pop! Pump, Pop! Pump and *Click!* he emptied the magazine. Turning to Jake he barked, 'What range did you sight your scope in for?

'Fifty metres.'

'Try seventy-five next time, your shot went low.'

'Is that right, Mister big-shot-with-the-open-sights? Well, let's just see how you did. I only saw one drop.'

After Wolf had eased himself back into the ute, Jake started the engine and drove to the left of the vineyard. Expecting to find one dead rabbit lying there, he jumped out and started running his feet through the knee-high grass, searching for the body, while Wolf watched from the ute's cab.

He saw Jake bend and then straighten with a shout of, 'Two!' Turning toward the car, he held up a pair of rabbits by their back legs.

Wolf pointed through the windscreen and called, 'Try a bit further to your right.'

Jake stopped and shook his head, but then obliged. When he almost stepped on another dead rabbit, he rolled his eyes and reluctantly collected the limp, still warm body. Placing the three carcasses in the back of the ute, he quipped, 'All head shots, you arsey bastard.'

Wolf dipped his head at the back-handed compliment. 'Guess they'll keep the dog fed for a coupl'a days.'

'Sebastian?' Jake gave a bark of laughter. 'The spoilt mutt only eats that "gourmet" shit out of a can. Nah, we'll have these for dinner tomorrow night. After all, they've been gettin' nice 'n fat off the farm.' He leaned on the sill of the driver's door and smiled in at Wolf. 'Hey, do you remember Dad showin' us how to make rabbit stew?'

'Actually … I do, and as a kid I didn't reckon it tasted half bad.' Wolf gave a lopsided grin. 'After we've skinned 'em, we'll soak 'em overnight in salt water to get the gamey taste out, like the old man used to.'

'Right you are.' Jake climbed into the driver's seat and reached over to thump his brother on the shoulder. 'Nice shootin', ace.'

'Thanks, mate.' After hesitating a moment Wolf added, 'Good to know I haven't lost that.'

'Yeah, and I'm bettin' in time everything'll come back t'ya.' Jake turned the key in the ignition and the diesel rumbled into life. Flicking Wolf a guilty glance, he mumbled, 'Oh, and Amber doesn't need to know I called Sebastian a mutt.'

'Don't worry.' Wolf threw him a wink. 'I've got your back.'

Smiling, Jake put the car into gear. 'I'll get the water pump goin', then how 'bout I take you for the grand tour? Not that the farm's changed much since we were kids….'

At the stomp of footsteps past her cabin door Modeen's eyes snapped open. As the sound receded she lay still, judging by her body clock that it was too early for another delivery of porridge from Boof. Putting her hands behind her head, she lay back to stare unseeingly into the dimness above her bunk.

This was her fifth morning on the trawler.

And something was different.

She'd grown accustomed to the boat's motion on the open water, its pitch, sway and yaw, but now it was travelling smoothly and its engine's note was a constant, even hum.

And then came more footsteps.

This time they stopped outside her door. She tensed as a key was thrust into the lock, and then the door was flung open and she was hit by the harsh beam of a torch. Squinting in the glare, she raised an arm to shield her eyes as a distinctive voice barked, 'Get up! We're moving you in fifteen minutes.'

The man with the silver buckle.

An instant later the door slammed shut again, footsteps marched off, and she was left in the quiet darkness once more. Muttering dourly under her breath, 'Thanks for the heads-up,' she slid her legs over the edge of the bunk and bent to put on her boots. Straightening, she ran her fingers through her hair and listened for movement outside the cabin. When all was quiet she lifted the head of the bunk's mattress, and with deft fingers retrieved the electrode she'd stashed there.

After securing the small but handy tool inside the lining of her combat boot, she lowered the mattress again.

When he opened her cabin door and shone the kerosene lamp inside, Boof found Modeen leaning against the bulkhead, her palms pressed flat against its cool surface, legs extended behind her in a classic full body stretch. He lifted the lamp higher and was relieved to see she was still securely chained by one wrist.

She turned to throw him a smile and a cheery, 'Morning Boof.'

He grunted in response. Keeping his eyes fixed on her, he placed the lamp on a ledge and gestured for her to turn around.

'Hands behind your back.'

When she complied, he proceeded to unlock the chain connecting her to the bulkhead and wrapped the end of it around her forearms. Then, after unclipping the chain from her handcuffs, he promptly cuffed her wrists together. Satisfied her hands were secured behind her back, he dropped the chain to the floor and took out a pillowslip, which he pulled over her head.

As he guided her out of the cabin and onto the main deck, Modeen heard the engine stop. The trawler slowed and then, with a loud squeak, the port side hull bumped against the fender of a solid mooring. Beside her Boof took a staggering step as the boat lurched to a complete halt. Her straining ears caught the lap of water against a shoreline, and through the pillowslip she glimpsed lights in the distance piercing the early morning darkness.

Boof's hand on her arm tightened as he growled, 'Stop,' and then she was lifted over a beefy shoulder. With a gruff, 'Don't try anything funny,' he stepped from the boat onto a stable surface. The wooden boards creaked under their combined weight as they traversed what she assumed to be a jetty. She counted thirty paces before he stopped and lowered her into the side of a van. A moment later she felt the vehicle sink low on its suspension as the big man climbed in next to her.

As he was sliding the door closed, she heard the man with the silver buckle shout, 'Take her to the shed.'

Boof paused, the van door still partly open. 'Aren't you coming, boss?'

'I'm going to see the Nakahi Pango,' came the curt

reply. 'And Boof, make sure you keep her tied up at all times. He wants her in one piece so don't let the guys play with her either.'

'Right, boss.'

With that, the door slammed closed and the van bounced forward, jolting Modeen onto her side. The cold metal floor offered little cushioning but she settled herself as best she could. After less then a minute she felt the vehicle slow, make a right turn, and come to a stop with its engine at idle. Outside, a metallic roller door groaned and rattled open, and then the van moved forward as the roller door creaked and banged to a close behind the vehicle.

Boof slid the door open and the van's suspension bounced upward as he got out. Modeen sat up without speaking, her every sense on high alert at the sound of approaching footsteps and a chorus of men's raised voices.

'Boof's back, and he's not alone!'

There was a long, drawn-out wolf whistle amid the commotion, followed by a suggestive, 'Hey hey hey! What have you brought us, Boof?'

When he snapped, 'Nothing for you,' another voice shouted, 'Come on, we won't hurt her.'

'If anyone touches her,' Boof growled, 'they'll answer to Nakahi Pango.' This extinguished their loud demands like water on a grass fire, although a few continued to mutter sullenly. But when he added with an air of menace, 'And if you know what's good for you, you'll make yourselves scarce,' the murmurs died as the crowd dispersed. 'Hey Needles,' Boof called to the man trailing the pack, 'give me a hand here.'

Reaching into the van, Boof pulled Modeen toward him across the floor. After once again hoisting her onto a brawny shoulder he carried her into the main chamber of the shed, where he set her down near one of the round metal columns supporting the roof. Using a length of rope, he bound her to the column and made certain she was secure before undoing one of her handcuffs. After threading her hands around the pole, he snapped the open cuff back on her wrist again. He obviously wasn't taking any chances, no doubt painfully aware of how handy she was.

She heard sounds of movement and then another, slimy voice close by said, 'Let's see your face.' A blast of foul smelling breath assaulted her senses as the pillowslip was whipped off her head. She squinted while her eyes adjusted to the floodlighting, and then swept a glance around the shed's interior.

It looked like a man cave. Its high corrugated iron ceiling was festooned with thick grey cobwebs, and stained and tattered sofas and armchairs were scattered around the concrete floor. A dartboard hung askew on one wall, its surface pockmarked beyond recognition and a few grimy, featherless darts hanging morosely from its bullseye.

To Modeen's right, a set of stairs built into the side of what appeared to be a small office and amenities unit led to a mezzanine floor above the office, where a group of six dark-skinned men sat smoking and playing cards around a battered circular table. To the left of them, another group of four were drinking and playing pool near a rustic bar. Beyond that, she could see an old Bongo van parked in front of a solid industrial roller door.

Her eyes narrowed and she refocused on the skinny guy with the bad breath and patchy five o'clock shadow who was standing in front of her holding the pillowslip. He let it fall to the floor and ran his tongue suggestively over chipped yellow teeth while slinking closer, blood-shot eyes raking over her.

'She's pretty.' His foul breath had her turning away and screwing up her nose in distaste, and his goofy grin revealed a mouthful of teeth only a money-hungry dentist could love.

Boof turned from undoing the rope around her and snarled, 'Get away from her Needles, ya little shit.'

'I'm not gonna hurt 'er,' the scrawny rat-like man said, licking his lips. As he spoke he stepped forward, hands outstretched as if to grope her breasts.

Still eyeing him with disgust, Modeen bunched herself against the pole and then lashed out, kicking him hard between the legs. He let out a high-pitched yelp as his knees gave way and he doubled over, clutching his groin.

WHACK!

His head snapped sideways as Modeen sent him to

the floor with a follow-up kick. He lay there in the foetal position, his breathing ragged and his face contorted with pain, while mocking laughter erupted from his watching colleagues.

Boof too was grinning. He moved to stand by Modeen's side and pointed a thick, meaty finger at Needles. 'Told ya to back off, didn't I.'

Needles' flushed face twisted with rage. When he leapt toward her, clenched fist raised, Modeen prepared to lash out again, but Boof stepped between them. He was twice Needles' size, so when he shoved him in the chest with an open palm, he sent the little man flying into a stockpile of empty two hundred litre oil drums on the other side of the shed. He didn't surface until after the drums had stopped wobbling and rolling, but his groans were clearly heard. When he finally dragged himself to his feet to limp into one of the back rooms, he kept his head down and gave Modeen and Boof a wide berth.

With a satisfied grunt, Boof dragged over a beat-up old sofa and settled back to keep watch on his prisoner. Above his head a dusty, cobwebbed clock sporting the iconic picture of Marilyn Monroe holding down a billowing white skirt, read o-four hundred hours. Modeen wondered if that was the right time. If so, it was the most gruelling hour of the night, a fact any nightshift worker would confirm. And Modeen had worked plenty of graveyard shifts both during her time with the SASR and as a security guard.

She remained still and quiet, and after a bit the men lost interest in her. Sliding down the pole into a squatting position, she crossed one leg under her butt and sat on it. Boof watched through heavy-lidded eyes as she tried a few positions, searching for the most comfortable. By the time she finally settled with her butt on the floor and her legs stretched in front of her, his head had nodded onto his chest and his eyes were battling to stay open.

She followed his lead, allowing her head to droop and her eyes to close, but she wasn't asleep. Having managed right under Boof's nose to retrieve the electrode from her boot, she was soundlessly and with as little movement as possible, going to work on her handcuffs.

The Marilyn clock said o-five hundred hours when Modeen raised her head. A glimmer of light crept into the shed through what she suspected was an obscured window above the mezzanine floor. She could see the men up there dozing at the table, heads resting on their folded arms. The others were on the ground floor, sprawled on sofas. There was no sound inside the shed except the steady drone of snores.

It was time to make her bid for freedom.

Moving silently, she bent her legs and positioned her feet beneath her. Bracing her back on the pole, she rose slowly to her feet, taking care not to make any noise. She stood for a moment, hands behind her back, and checked the room.

No change to the snore rhythms.

No one had stirred.

Slipping the handcuff off her left wrist, she clipped it to the one on her right so it wouldn't flail about and jangle as she moved, and then tiptoed toward the front service door.

I'll remove the handcuffs later.

The door, situated to the right of the office, offered a blind spot from the rest of the shed's occupants. She checked again that no one had stirred before reaching out to grab the door handle ... only to find there wasn't one.

Damn, they've removed it!

She paused to consider her options. Needles was in the back room, so it would be her last resort. Slipping under the staircase, she tried the office.

The window's barred.

The one in the loo?

Barred.

The kitchen window?

There isn't one.

She paused, frowning.

Now I know why they were so casual about going to sleep. I'm locked in here with them.

A heightened sense of urgency rose within her.

The roller door.

She turned and crept across the room to where the

Bongo van sat in front of the roller door. Searching for the electric control panel, she found it beside the door. It had one button for up, one for down and a red Emergency Stop. About to hit the Up button, she recalled the racket the door made when moving, and readied herself.

Hit the button and squat on the other side of the Bongo. The door only has to rise three hundred millimetres for me to slide under it and be gone.

Taking one last look around the shed and finding all still quiet, she jammed her thumb on the Up button and steeled herself.

Nothing happened.

What the —?

Slipping around to the other side of the roller door, she saw chains dangling from the top of the roller mechanism.

Guess I'll just have to open it manually … great.

She grasped the chain in both hands and put all her weight on it, but it wouldn't budge. Letting go of the chain, she stared at the mechanism and frowned.

Need to disconnect the roller.

That was when she noticed the lever had been snapped off. She was still staring at its useless nub when a yell of, 'BOOF! She's loose!' came from above. She whipped around to see one of the two men on the mezzanine floor gesturing wildly in her direction.

The mezzanine floor window!

As she raced across the room, not bothering to move stealthily this time, all the shed's occupants began to stir.

Seeing her running toward them, the men on the mezzanine floor moved to the top of the staircase landing and braced themselves. Three quarters of the way up the stairs she stopped and flung herself backward. Twisting her body in mid-air, she grabbed hold of the horizontal bar spanning the stairwell. With all the grace of an elite gymnast, she kicked forward, powering through the swing to gain as much height and momentum as she could. On the return swing she flexed, driving herself backward. Thrusting her body high and tucking in her legs, she straightened and stood vertically on the bar. With her arms outstretched for balance, she pivoted to her right, grasped the top railing surrounding the mezzanine floor, and vaulted over it.

Bounding forward she landed a heavy side kick on the window, all her weight behind the blow. The force sent her rebounding backward as louvers shattered ... against a set of sturdy metal bars.

More bars, damn it! I'll have to find another way out.

She whipped around and saw the two men from the landing skirting around the table toward her. She sprang forward and the first man went down from a spinning back kick to the side of his head. The other tried rushing her, and was sent over her shoulder with a smoothly executed judo throw. Straightening, she made for the stairs. A crowd had formed at its base and two more men were on their way up.

She didn't stop, meeting them halfway with a powerful stomp to the chest of the first man and sending him careering backward onto the man behind. Grabbing the top rail of the staircase, she vaulted over the side and onto the concrete floor below, where Boof and the rest of the men advanced on her. Four and then five of them spread out in front of her, pushing her back toward the door. Needles emerged from the back room to join them, and this time he was armed.

Taking up position to her left, he pulled out a pair of nan chucks and twirled one of the batons in front of him like a propeller, taunting, 'You're gonna to get it now, gorgeous.'

Modeen leapt at him, intercepting the spinning baton and wrenching the nan chucks from his grip. She pirouetted to her right, slamming the free baton into the forehead of the guy beside Needles. Spinning back, she took out Needles with a backhand blow as the twirling baton cracked him in the side of the temple. Both men slumped to the floor as the baton came to a stop and Modeen turned to face the rest of her attackers.

When another man stepped toward her, she set the batons whirling again until they were a frenzied blur of motion slicing through the air around her torso. She brought them to a stop, one baton neatly tucked under an arm, her free hand extended forward and her opposite leg back in a classic Bruce Lee stance. She stood there poised, daring her attacker to take another step forward.

The man frowned, indecisive, and then growled, 'Frig this.' As he pulled a Glock from his waistband, a baton whipped out and CRACK! the knuckle of his hand shattered as the pistol was knocked to the floor. He cried out in pain and backed away cradling his injured hand, as the man to his right came at Modeen. Stepping forward and using the back swing of the baton, she struck him under the chin. The force of the blow smashed teeth and sent him backward with an agonised howl.

Bringing the baton to a halt under her arm while bending to retrieve the Glock, she pointed the gun at each of them in turn. 'Back, all of you.' When they complied, she tilted her head toward the door behind her and said pleasantly, 'Now Boof, you're going to open the door for me.'

'No, he's not.'

THWACK!

Two electrodes struck her squarely in the back. As her muscles contracted and her body convulsed, she fired off a shot into the air. It ricocheted uselessly through the structure as she fell to the floor. Lying there, twitching and cursing herself for not having heard his stealthy entrance, she could only watch as the man with the silver buckle swaggered up to stand over her. He pointed the Taser at her face, smirked, and released the trigger.

CHAPTER SIXTEEN

Wolf was sitting up in bed when the door to his room moved a fraction and then swung inward. A black button nose appeared around it, followed by a brown and white face as the Shih Tzu slipped into the room, blue satin ribbon on top of its fluffy head bobbing with each step. Catching sight of the man scowling down at it from the bed, the little dog stopped in its tracks to stare at him with wary, bulging eyes.

At Wolf's gravelly, 'What're you lookin' at?' the dog hurriedly backed away, trembling. In its haste it fell onto its haunches and briefly squatted on the spot before dashing out of the room, tail pressed against its back legs. Seeing the spreading wet patch on the carpet left in its wake, Wolf screwed up his nose in disgust and muttered, *'Great,'* just as a rap came on the open door.

He called gruffly, 'Yeah?' and Jake walked in.

'I see Sebastian came to say good morning.' Jake's expression was guarded, anticipating a backlash.

Wolf growled, 'It came in, pissed on the carpet, and bolted.'

Sighing, 'Sounds about right,' Jake gave a resigned shake of his dark head. 'Amber will clean that up. Now, on a more cheery note, how'd you like a spot of fishin' this mornin'?'

Wolf's expression lifted. 'Sure.'

'Excellent, we'll go after breakfast. I'll bring the car 'round the front again.' As he turned to leave, Jake took care to step around the wet patch, throwing Wolf a doleful backward glance as he did so.

'You're improving.' Jake watched his brother lift his legs into the passenger side of the work ute.

'Y'reckon?'

'Yeah. For one thing, this morning you got Amber's name right first time.' Jake flashed him a teasing grin and started the ute.

'Humph.' Wolf raised one eyebrow and then frowned. 'But I do feel like I've made progress. I've cut back on the painkillers and I don't need to use those damn crutches as much. And working out with your dumbbells is helping me get my upper body strength back.'

'You always did like workin' out 'til you felt the

burn.' Jake put the ute into gear and it bumped into motion.

Wolf's frown deepened as he settled himself in the seat. 'Yeah, but I won't be runnin' any marathons just yet, my legs still feel lethargic.'

'Take it easy, bro, don't try to rush things. I'm actually startin' to enjoy havin' you around.' Jake threw him a lop-sided grin.

Wolf merely nodded and turned to gaze out the window, but Jake caught the hint of a smile at the corner of his mouth.

A short while later they pulled in close to the river bank and Jake turned off the ignition. 'I've still got the old dinghy.'

Wolf eyed the small aluminium boat. 'Doesn't look too bad for such an old tinny.'

'I've had to make a few mods to it over the years.'

Nodding his approval, Wolf climbed out of the ute. 'Ya know, I haven't eaten trout for as long as I can remember … although that isn't sayin' much,' and he gave a wry snort, 'seein' as how there's a whole lot I don't remember.'

Jake lifted the tackle box and fishing rods out of the ute's rear tray while Wolf hobbled his way to the dinghy. Following him to the water's edge, Jake called, 'Reckon we might do better then trout today.' At Wolf's curious glance, he tapped the side of his nose with a finger. 'Got me some inside information. There's been a breach in one of the nets at the salmon ponds downstream. With a bit of luck we got ourselves some prime Atlantic salmon escapees headin' this way.'

'So what are we waitin' for?'

Jake held the boat stable while his brother climbed laboriously in and plonked himself with a grunt on the metal bench seat up front. After stashing the rods and tackle box on the floor at the back of the boat, Jake trekked up to the ute again and returned carrying a twelve volt battery and container of outboard fuel.

'Sorry I couldn't help ya lug the gear.'

Bending to connect the fuel to the motor Jake puffed, 'Don't worry. You can repay me later when you're at full capacity again.' He threw Wolf a grin.

'What's the battery for?'

'You don't remember?'

'Remember what?'

'You'll see.' Throwing the anchor onto the floor of the boat, Jake pushed the dinghy off the bank and jumped in. After pumping the primer a couple of times, he went to work on the pull cord.

As the motor chugged lethargically into life Wolf muttered, 'Sounds like it's time to change those plugs.'

Jake's lips twitched. 'I'll add that to the list of jobs you'll be tackling later.' He shrugged. 'Don't get to use the boat much, the farm keeps me too busy.' He rapped on the throttle and the spinning propeller dug deep in the water, thrusting the bow of the dinghy into the air before the boat settled on the plane. As they motored down a wide section of river, Jake connected his portable fish finder and GPS, turned it on and handed it to Wolf. 'Let me know if you see anything interesting.'

'Where we headin'?'

'The trusted "Secret Spot" where Dad used to take us when we were kids. Do ya remember?' Jake didn't wait before going on. 'The deep drop-off near the riverbank, under that big old willow tree you and I used to climb when we got bored with fishin'.' He raised one eyebrow. 'And if I remember rightly, you pushed me off that tree and into the drink.'

Wolf looked up from the GPS screen. 'Yeah, that's something I *do* remember. Recall enjoyin' it too.'

'And you did it more than once.'

Wolf gave a bark of laughter. 'Just teachin' you to swim.'

'And to watch my back.'

'Both important lessons for a young bloke to learn.'

They shared a moment of amused nostalgia and then Jake said, 'Not far now.'

As they neared the spot Wolf held up an arm, fist clenched in a commando-style halt gesture.

Jake said drily, 'Good thing I know what that means, thanks to you and Dad,' and cut the motor.

Still gazing at the screen, Wolf announced, 'Multiple signals ahead, coming this way ... big ones too.'

With a smug, 'Got some new lures for just such an

occasion,' Jake handed Wolf a fishing rod. 'Cast out to where you think they might be.'

'They're movin' quickly and headin' up stream.' Wolf had the eager glint of a hunter in his eyes. 'Gotta be salmon.'

When an hour later the expected good catch hadn't eventuated, Wolf gave a disdainful sniff. 'Y'know what you can do with these new lures....'

Jake shrugged. 'Maybe the fish are still comin'.'

Taking a glance at the GPS Wolf shook his head and growled, 'Nah, there's been a steady stream of the buggars passin' right by us. Any other time I'd jump in and just *grab* one.' He swore loudly and punched one of his legs with a frustrated fist.

Seeing that, Jake began reeling in his line. 'Well, I guess it's time we resort to the old man's fail-safe method.'

Wolf stared at him and then frowned. 'You still got some of his old dets?'

'No, but Uncle Ralph gave me some of his stash when he left the coal mine.'

Wolf watched him wire up a detonator to a roll of twin core cable, mumbling doubtfully, 'That thing looks like it's passed its use-by date.'

'They're all like this.'

'Aren't you worried about 'em goin' off after all these years?'

'Nah, they're more likely to be duds. The last ones I tried were. So we might have to give this a coupl'a goes.' Making a loop in the cable near the detonator, Jake clipped on a sinker and then dropped the det over the side. Picking up the oars, he rowed to what he estimated to be a safe distance while Wolf reeled out the twin core cable behind them. When Jake stopped rowing, Wolf handed him the reel.

After twitching the black wire to the negative side of the twelve volt battery, Jake said, 'You ready?'

'Wait.' Wolf was checking the fish finder. 'Wait,' he said again, and then, 'OK, let 'er rip!'

As Jake pressed the red wire to the positive electrode there was a second's delay and then …

BOOM!

Water erupted into the air and then fell, showering the occupants of the dinghy which shook violently in the water. Jake gave a rousing whoop and gripped both sides of the boat to steady himself. Chuckling, 'That was no dud!' he shook the water off his head, but the laughter died in his throat when he caught sight of his brother.

Wolf's whole body had convulsed at the moment of impact. Jake watched, horrified, as his jaw clenched and his eyes rolled back in his head. When a large wave, radiating from the centre of the explosion hit the dinghy, tossing it back and sideways, Wolf fell forward, banging his head and shoulders against the centre bench seat. And when the boat finally stopped rocking, he remained sprawled across the seat, his breathing ragged, his body rigid.

Jake dropped to his knees beside him and shook him by a shoulder. 'You alright, bro?'

Wolf moaned and stirred, blinking and making fists with both hands. He shook his head as though trying to clear it. 'The chopper,' he ground out, grabbing Jake's shoulder in a vice-like grip. 'Bugs, the chopper!' His voice rose. 'Take it *out!*' Then his face contorted with shock and dread. His hand slipped from Jake's shoulder as he jerked upright with an agonised shout of, 'Jo!' His eyes were open but wild, unseeing. He gripped the edge of the seat with white-knuckled hands and bellowed, 'JO! *JO!*'

The last bellow was more like a howl to Jake's startled ears. Seeing Wolf's eyes glaze over and his head tilt backward, Jake leapt toward him, catching him before he could slump to the deck again. Murmuring, 'It's alright, Troy. Take it easy, mate,' he lowered him to the floor and shoved a rolled towel under his head. Once he was still, Jake carefully thumbed open one of his eyelids.

When all he could see were the whites of his brother's eyes, he let loose a string of expletives. Whipping around, he yanked on the outboard's pull cord. The instant the motor coughed into life he gave it full throttle, powering the dinghy into a sweeping U-turn. As it rose to the plane its rear gunwale dipped low, putting Jake close to the churning water. Out of the corner of an eye he glimpsed a silver flash and recognised the shape.

With Wolf's words ringing in his ears, he thrust a hand into the water and scooped up the stunned salmon. Dropping the fish unceremoniously to the floor beside him, he made sure the throttle was on full and leaned forward as the boat sped to the shore.

After running the bow of the dinghy hard up onto the bank, he dragged Wolf's heavy, unresponsive body out and onto the grass. Not waiting to catch his breath, Jake checked his brother's breathing and pulse before rushing to the waterline again. He hurried back, dripping towel in his hands, to drop to his knees. After squeezing most of the water out of the towel, he used it to wipe Wolf's forehead.

Should I call an ambulance or drive him to the hospital?

He's breathing normally and he has a strong pulse....

He was still anxiously running through the options in his head when Wolf gave a drawn-out groan and blinked. Jake sat back, blowing his relief through pursed lips.

As Wolf's vision cleared, he frowned incredulously at his brother and croaked, 'Jake?'

Smiling, Jake shook his head. 'Oh man, you scared the *crap* outta me.'

The words were barely out of his mouth when Wolf sucked in a breath and sat bolt upright. Wincing at the sudden movement, he ran a hand over his face.

'You need to take it easy, bro. You just had a nasty turn—' Jake stopped to stare open-mouthed at his brother, who was mumbling something about a phone and feverishly patting all the pockets in his cargo pants.

When his search came up empty, he turned angst-ridden eyes on Jake. 'Where's my mobile?'

'Back at the house, mate, same as mine.' When Wolf's expression darkened, Jake added, 'The reception's crap down here by the river, and we were supposed to be here to catch fish, not make phone calls or send texts.'

Wolf snaked out a hand to grab him by the arm, saying through tight lips, 'I have to make an urgent call. Can you take me home right now?'

Jake frowned and stared into his face. 'Sure you're OK?'

'I will be once you get me home.' Wolf was already struggling to his feet.

Jake helped him up. 'Alright....'

Wolf didn't speak again on the trip home. Concerned, Jake glanced at him occasionally and each time found him sitting quietly staring out the window with a faraway look in his eyes. Even before Jake had brought the ute to a stop outside the homestead, Wolf had undone his seatbelt and opened the passenger-side door.

'Hang on Troy, I'll help you.'

With a gruff, 'I can manage,' Wolf climbed down from the ute and began hobbling toward the house. Once inside he made an unsteady beeline for his room, where his eyes fell on the mobile Ben had given him, sitting where he'd left it on the bedside table. Moving as quickly as he could, he hurried over to grab it and straightaway dialled the only number in the contact list.

As soon as the call was answered he barked, 'Ben. Where's Jo?'

After a brief pause Ben said, 'Wolf?'

'Yeah it's me, now where's Jo?'

Ben paused again before asking, 'What do you remember, Wolf?'

'Everything.'

'Humour me.'

Wolf rolled his eyes and blurted, 'Julia Creek, the chopper, Reger, Foster, the explosion ... like I just said, *everything.*'

'I see.' During the pregnant pause that followed Wolf was about to prompt him when Ben said carefully, 'JD's missing, Wolf.'

'Missing?'

'We believe ... taken.'

'*Taken?*' Realising how loud his voice had become Wolf swallowed and said more calmly, 'Taken where and by who?' He heard the frustration in Ben's reply.

'We don't have any details as yet, at this point we're working on leads and hunches.'

'I don't understand ... you can track her so you must know where she is.'

Ben sighed. 'It's complicated.'

'So *uncomplicate* it for me.' Even to his own ears Wolf's tone was harsh, demanding.

That fact wasn't lost on Ben. He said evenly, 'You

sound stressed, Wolf, and that can't be good for your recovery. Maybe I should have a word with Jake—'

'No ... wait.' Wolf hung his head, struggling to rein in his surging emotions. Finally he said, 'Sorry, Ben, I didn't mean to yell at you. I'm just worried about Jo.'

'And I know how you feel, mate ... better than most.'

Recalling how Ben's wife and daughter had been kidnapped and the team's successful rescue of them, Wolf exhaled and said in a more normal voice, 'Can't you at least tell me how you lost track of her?'

'When you were injured,' Ben began slowly, 'and the prognosis for your recovery was ... not promising ... it affected JD badly.' He paused. 'She went rogue, Wolf. Removed her tracker so we couldn't follow her movements.'

'Rogue?' The crease deepened in Wolf's brow. 'Why would she do that?'

'I guess seeing you in intensive care was more than she could handle. And when she discovered that Reger had escaped the Julia Creek siege, she went in pursuit and ... neutralised him. But she didn't stop there. She started taking out key members of the Black Mamba's hierarchy. We don't know this for sure but we suspect that's why she's been taken.'

'Why didn't you stop her?'

'She wouldn't listen to me, or anyone else for that matter.'

'But you're her boss—'

'She resigned from NatSec, Wolf.'

Neither man spoke for a long moment.

Wolf finally said, 'But you're actively looking for her, right?'

'Of course. I even pulled Bugs and Spooky off another case to work on it.' Ben waited, knowing what was coming next.

'I want in, Ben.'

Recalling his own feelings when his family was taken, Ben kept his tone calm and even when he said, 'I know you do, but you've only just been released from hospital after coming out of a coma. You can't even walk unaided, how could I deem you fit enough to go on a mission when you're still recuperating?'

'I can walk, Ben ... and I can still shoot.'

'Well that's good news of course, but it still wouldn't justify my taking you off leave prematurely. Jack would have my hide! He's already on my back about reassigning the other two guys.'

Wolf clutched the ring dangling from the chain around his neck. 'Please ... I *need* to find her.' He realised he was begging, a new low for him, but in this case he didn't care.

'I'd rather you were giving yourself time to heal.' Ben's voice wavered, his resolve severely tested by his friend's entreaty. Tapping on his phone, he zoomed in on Wolf's tracker.

Good, he's still in Tasmania.

'Ben?' The sharp edge in Wolf's voice clinched it.

Ben gave a resigned sigh. 'Look, we suspect she's

been taken to En-Zed. If you can get yourself to Auckland you'll be close if anything eventuates. I'd organise your flights but Jack's made it clear he's watching this case with keen interest and he wouldn't sanction your travel. Duty of care and all that.'

'No problem.' The relief in Wolf's voice was almost tangible.

'And Wolf,' Ben went on sternly, 'that's the best I can do for now.'

'Thanks. At least I'll be doing *something*.'

'Don't thank me, I'm not doing you any favours. We both know you should be resting up, not taking part in a mission before you're fully recovered.'

'Well in my book you *are* doing me a favour, Ben.' Wolf ended the call and turned to see Jake standing in the doorway. Their eyes locked and then Wolf mumbled, 'You heard?'

'Just the last bit, about you taking part in some "mission".' Jake shook his head and stepped further into the room. 'Did I hear right? You're going to *New Zealand?*' When the only response he got was a silent, impassive stare, Jake threw his hands in the air. 'In your condition? After what happened on the river?'

Wolf regarded him steadily. 'I am.'

'Are you out of your *mind?* And what the *hell* is your boss thinking, sending you on some mission?'

'He's not *sending* me, he's just suggesting I could be of help, that's all.'

'Help to who? Not yourself, obviously.'

Wolf sighed. 'Look, I know you're doing this 'cos you care about me, Jake, but I don't have time to argue. Just believe me when I tell you I *have* to go.'

Jake's shoulders slumped and he gave a frustrated snort. 'You're pullin' the big brother routine on me again, just like you always do.'

'No, I'm just asking you to trust me.' Seeing Wolf bend and attempt to drag his khaki duffel out from under the bed, Jake hastened to help.

'I can't talk you out of this?'

'No.' It was Jake's turn to sigh as Wolf went on. 'I'll book the next available flights when I get to the airport. Can you drop me there?'

'What, now?'

'Yes, now.'

On the drive to Hobart International Airport, Wolf sat staring out the window deep in thought. The silence eventually got to Jake.

'So … you've got everything you need?'

Wolf nodded.

'What about something to read on the plane? Got a book?'

Wolf frowned and then his eyes widened. Reaching into the back seat, he dug a paperback out of his duffel.

Glimpsing the book's cover, Jake said, 'I thought you finished that one?'

Muttering absently, 'I did,' Wolf flicked to the back

cover. The message scribbled there hadn't made sense when he first saw it … but it did now.

Troy, the answer to your question is 'yes'.

With love,

Mrs Ryan

A message from Modeen! Left when he was in the coma.

I knew I kept that book for a reason.

He let his eyes linger over her handwriting and then snapped the book shut and slipped it back into his duffel.

Jake was distracted by the traffic for a bit and then piped up again. 'I guess you remember how you ended up in hospital now?' When his brother didn't answer straightaway, Jake gave a cynical snort. 'Don't tell me, that's classified, right?'

This time Wolf turned to fix him with a solemn gaze. 'We were on a mission,' he said quietly, 'and Jo got into a bit of strife. I was running to help her and … got blown up for my troubles.'

Jake's eyes were drawn to Wolf's hand, which was fingering the ring on the chain around his neck. 'And what's the story with that?'

Wolf looked down at it and then back at his brother with a pained expression. 'Right before that mission I … um … asked Jo to … well … marry me.'

Jake's mouth dropped open. '*Marry* you? Wow, wait 'til I tell Amber! We thought you'd never settle down.'

He gave an awed shake of his head before adding drily, 'But how's your timing, bro?'

'Yeah, that's what Jo said too. Anyway, that was the last time I saw this,' and Wolf waved the ring in the air, ''til I woke up in hospital with it around *my* neck for some reason.'

Jake paused while he took it all in, and then said, 'So, can I ask why the trip to New Zealand?'

'I'm going to help with the search.'

'Search?'

'For Jo. She's gone missing.'

'So that's why she hasn't been around.' Jake pulled up in front of the airport terminal and turned to Wolf, indicating the ring around his neck with a lift of his chin. 'I hope that's not her way of saying no to your proposal, bro,' he said solemnly.

Wolf exhaled through tight lips. 'Or that she's changed her mind.'

CHAPTER SEVENTEEN

'At Papakura Military Base,' Bugs said into his phone, 'just awaiting orders.'

'Are you mobile?'

'Yeah, Ben, kitted out 'n ready to roll.'

'Good,' Ben said crisply. 'Surveillance picked up the Mamba's second in command leaving their Auckland stronghold around o-four thirty this morning, and followed him to a warehouse on River Road in Dargaville. Stand-by, I'll send you the coordinates and a picture of the man in question.'

A few seconds later Bug's phone pinged with an incoming text. He clicked on the attachment and brought up a picture of a solidly-built Maori in a black V-neck tee shirt and straight-leg jeans. The shirt was stretched over an impressively muscular chest. Handing the phone to Spooky, Bugs nudged the Humvee into gear.

After studying the photo, Spooky gave a long whistle. 'How's the silver buckle on this dude.' He was about to hand the phone back to Bugs when it buzzed with an incoming call.

'Get that, will ya?' Bugs muttered as he powered the Humvee through the gears.

Glancing at the caller ID Spooky announced, 'It's the wolfman!' He pressed Answer and Speaker so Bugs could hear the conversation as well. 'Wolfman!' he said jubilantly, 'how're ya travelin', buddy?'

'Better. Got my memory back and comin' good.'

'That's brilliant, mate!'

'So I wanna be brought up to speed on the mission.'

The two men in the Humvee shared a meaningful glance and then Spooky said, 'Ben mentioned you'd be getting in contact. Where are you?'

'Hobart Airport, on my way to NZ. The best I could get is a six hour flight, via Melbourne. What about you guys?'

'Auckland, about to follow up on another lead. If it checks out we might have some good news for ya. Give us a call when you land.'

'Roger.'

When Modeen's body stopped convulsing she blinked and tried to steady her breathing. Lying face-up, she could feel the two Taser electrodes digging into her back. She willed her body to roll over but it refused to obey, remaining prone, rigid, *useless*. At her frustrated grunt, a voice nearby sneered, 'You must like being Tasered. Let me know when you're ready for another round. Always happy to oblige.' The man with the silver buckle turned to Boof, his smirk replaced by a frown. 'I thought I told you to keep her tied up at all times?'

'Sorry boss, I thought she was.' Boof bent to clip her handcuffs back on.

'They didn't work the first time, what makes you think they're going to work now?' The man with the silver buckle flicked Modeen a contemptuous glance. 'Quite the female Houdini, aren't you?' Reaching into a back pocket, he said, 'Try these,' and handed Boof a pair of heavy-duty shackles and an allen key. 'No way she'll be able to unlock those babies.'

When Boof rolled her onto her side Modeen breathed out with relief at having the pressure taken off the barbs in her back. After examining the custom shackles, noting the quarter inch hi-tensile screws recessed deep into the body of the locking mechanism making them difficult – if not impossible – to remove without the proper tool, Boof gave an approving nod and used the allen key to open them. He then proceeded to pull her arms behind her back and fasten the shackles around her wrists, nipping them up tight.

The man with the silver buckle removed the electrode cartridge from the front of the X26C Taser in his hand and let it drop to the floor. Tucking the weapon into the front waistband of his jeans he barked, 'Bring the vehicles around. We're moving her to the city.'

Modeen felt two small tugs as the electrodes were yanked from her back. Boof flicked them to the side and rolled her onto her stomach, grabbing her around the neck with a large meaty hand. He sat her up and then lifted her onto his shoulder, to follow the six men heading for the Bongo van. They piled into the vehicle, two up front and the other four in the spacious cargo section.

The man with the silver buckle snapped, 'Where's Needles?'

'Over there, boss.'

'Needles!'

The prone man didn't move.

'Needles!'

Still nothing.

Rolling his eyes, the man with the silver buckle growled, 'Someone go wake him up.'

One of the other men jogged over to nudge Needles with a boot. When there was no response he did it again, harder, before announcing, 'He's dead, boss.'

With a callous, 'Leave him,' silver buckle motioned to Boof. 'C'mon, we're wasting time.'

With Modeen still on his shoulder, Boof flicked a switch behind the roller door control box and then hit the UP button. As soon as the door rattled open the Bongo reversed out, replaced seconds later by a black Ford Transit. The van's sliding door was thrown open and

Modeen was unceremoniously dumped inside. She fell back onto a warm body and looked down to see a man with his head covered by a black pillowslip. Another prisoner.

Whispering, 'Who are you?' she wriggled, trying to move her weight off him.

'ASIO,' came the muffled reply.

Modeen frowned. 'ASIO?' Then her expression lifted. 'Have you called it in?'

The pillowslip moved up and down. 'Yeah, help is on the way.'

BANG!

The agent's head rocked back against the floor of the van, blood pooling darkly in the pillowslip, as the sound of the gunshot resonated harshly inside the vehicle.

'No it's not,' the man with the silver buckle said smoothly, tucking the nine millimetre Glock back into his waistband. 'Now cover her,' he barked, 'and let's move.'

Modeen felt the van's suspension strain as Boof and two other men climbed into the cargo section with her, then a pillowslip was thrown over her head and the inside of the van went dark.

———

Salty put a comforting hand on Hannah's shoulder. 'I'm sure wherever she is, that niece of yours is alright, she's a very capable young lady. And young people can be impulsive … dropping everything and dashing off if something takes their fancy.'

'But it's so unlike Jo not to answer her phone, or at least call me back.' Hannah's eyes filled with tears.

He pulled her in for a hug. 'Come on, love, don't worry yourself into a tizz. I'm sure everything's OK.'

Hannah drew away to gaze up at him. 'But you don't understand, Richard. I *know* something's going on. She makes out like she's still in the Army, but I'm not stupid. Apart from her old khaki duffel there's no military gear here at all,' and she indicated Modeen's apartment with a sweep of her arm. 'No fatigues in the wash basket, not even a dress uniform hanging in her wardrobe. And the last time I recall seeing her polishing boots was about four years ago. No,' and she gave an emphatic shake of her grey head, 'she's mixed up in something else, and I'm starting to think it's something even more dangerous.'

'Ya know,' Salty said brightly, 'I've met her friends, and I can tell you they wouldn't let anything bad happen to her, no matter what she's up to. Besides, you might be worrying for nothing. She could simply be away on a field trip and out of mobile range.'

Hannah shook her head again. 'She didn't mention any field trip to me, only said she was in Hobart visiting Troy … who I suspect is more than just the "friend" she makes him out to be.' She gave a thoughtful frown. 'And I'd like to know how he ended up in hospital. Was she there when he got injured, maybe in danger herself?' Her voice rose. 'I need to talk to her!' Squeezing her eyes shut she cried, 'Why can't I reach her? Where *is* she?'

Salty took both her hands in a firm grip. 'You're letting your imagination run away with you, love. Didn't you tell me Josephine was the first woman to be accepted into the SASR, Australia's elite Special Forces?'

Hannah sniffed, swallowed and gave a teary nod.

'Well, you know they do some pretty dangerous things like jumping out of planes, getting shot out of torpedo tubes, not to mention special ops in war zones. So I think you should give that niece of yours some credit, she's well able to take care of herself.'

Grabbing a tissue to wipe her nose, Hannah murmured through it, 'I guess you're right.'

'That's my girl, think positive.' Slipping an arm around her shoulders, Salty gave her a squeeze. 'Now, how about I make us a coffee?'

Hannah rose to her feet. 'I'll do it, I need to stay busy.'

Salty watched her make her way into the kitchen. Then he opened the sliding glass doors and slipped out onto the balcony. Taking care to close the doors again, he took out his mobile and dialled Ben.

'Salty? I was just about to call you.'

'With an update on our young lady I hope?'

'We still haven't made contact with her,' Ben replied gravely, 'but I'm hopeful that we're closing in. Now, I need to ask another favour of you.'

'I'm listening.'

'Any chance you could fly to Auckland? I need a minder for Troy Wolverton.'

'Troy? But isn't he in hospital?'

'He's out now and in recovery. He's also determined to help us find JD.'

Salty rubbed his chin. 'That's understandable.'

'Yeah, but he's not fully recovered so I'm hoping you'll help me keep him out of trouble.'

After a pause Salty said, 'I haven't worked closely with the young fella before, so this'd give me a chance to get to know him better. Besides, I've got a vested interest in getting the little lady back.'

'Her aunt Hannah?'

'Right, and that's only one of the reasons. So, all things considered, I'll be glad to help out. And if there's anything else I can do, you go right ahead and ask me.'

'Thanks Salty.' Ben went on, 'I'm hoping we'll have this event wrapped up by the time you and Troy arrive in Auckland, but in case it's not, I'll send you information on what we have so far. Maybe you can keep Wolf busy going over the details to see if we've missed anything. Are you staying in JD's apartment on the Gold Coast?'

'Yep.'

'Right, I'll get Leanne to contact you with your flight details.'

———

Early morning frost turned the Ford Transit a dull charcoal-grey as it motored south along State Highway One. It passed through Paparoa heading toward Kaiwaka, where green rolling hills and patches of radiata pine trees gave way to thick undergrowth and tree-lined streets. They had just crossed the Kaiwaka River when the man with the silver buckle turned the van off the highway and pulled into a service station.

As the vehicle came to an abrupt stop Modeen was forced backward, against the ASIO agent's body. She grimaced at the corpse's cold rigidity after the hour-long trip.

The man with the silver buckle remained at the wheel, throwing Boof a curt nod. As the big man jumped out to fill the tank, a Bongo van pulled in behind and waited its turn at the bowser.

A minute later Boof's face appeared through the passenger's side window. Saying urgently, 'Boss,' he tilted his chin toward the highway.

The man with the silver buckle bent his head, muttering, 'I see 'em.'

'D'ya think—?'

'Just act casual,' came the brusque reply.

Taking care to keep his face in shadow, Boof finished fuelling the van, while on the road the camouflage-coloured Humvee roared past, its two occupants gazing intently ahead.

· · ·

An hour later the Humvee pulled onto the wide verge on River Road and Bugs announced, 'Place is deserted.'

'Yeah ... not looking too promising.' Spooky checked his mobile. 'But these are the coordinates Ben gave us.' He looked up and frowned. 'The ASIO agent was supposed to be waiting for us right here.'

'Well, it's still early and there aren't many people around. Let's check it out.' Bugs nosed the Humvee further up the road and then pulled into a small industrial complex. He swept a glance over the medium-sized workshops. 'Which shed?'

Spooky consulted his phone again. 'Keep going, it should be the last one on our right.' They crawled forward until he said, 'Stop here.' Eyeing the building, he rattled off a report, 'The front door looks solid enough ... bars on the bottom window.' He glanced up at the roof line. 'The top window's been smashed, recently too judging by all the glass on the ground.'

'What d'ya reckon?'

'Let's not stuff around. Grab those heavy bolt cutters out'the back and we'll go in through the bottom window.'

Bugs was out before he finished speaking and moments later they were inside the building.

After a quick sweep of the interior Bugs pointed to the floor next to a round metal column. 'Look here.' When Spooky hurried to his side Bugs muttered, 'See how the dust's been disturbed? Looks like someone was tied to this column.'

Spooky squatted to peer at the floor. 'Whoever it was, they were wearing combat boots.'

Bugs flashed a wry grin. 'What d'ya mean, *who?*' and Spooky chuckled.

'Yeah, you're right. This scene's got Modeen written all over it.' He pointed toward a corner. 'Looks like there was a big scuffle. There's a guy over there with his head caved in – by the nan chucks on the floor beside him I'd reckon – and upstairs near the smashed window it appears our combat-booted friend had another little rumble before leaping over the stairs.'

'You're a natural at this tracking gig aren't ya, mate?'

'Just makin' the most of my Special Forces training.'

They shared a grin and then Bugs sobered. 'This place is set up more like a clubhouse than a workshop.'

'I'll call it in.' Spooky took out his phone and dialled Ben.

About to take a final circuit of the premises, Bugs said, 'You might wanna mention that the ASIO agent didn't show.' A few minutes later, having finished his sweep, he joined Spooky again.

'Ben said there were two ASIO agents,' Spooky informed him. 'One was assigned to monitor the Mamba's main headquarters in Auckland city and the other was at the docks, on the lookout for a trawler.' He paused before adding, 'Looks like the vessel has resurfaced. Ben's had the agent at the docks recalled – doesn't want another ASIO dude goin' missing – and he wants us to check out the trawler. Throw me the keys, I'll drive us back.'

'Roger.' Bugs tossed him the Humvee keys. 'Hey, my blood sugar's gettin' low, so if we pass a dairy on the way how about we stop to grab a Coke or a coffee?'

'Dairy?' Spooky threw him a quizzical frown. 'I thought they only did milk and butter, that sort of stuff. Since when do they sell coffees?'

'That's what Kiwis call a convenience store.'

'Oh, right.'

They made their way outside and climbed back into the Humvee. As he accelerated away from the complex Spooky turned to Bugs. 'So what do Kiwis call a *real* dairy?'

CHAPTER EIGHTEEN

Modeen felt the van's rocking movement slow as the rumble of traffic outside grew louder and more constant. She knew they must be within city limits … but which city? She estimated they'd been on the road for two and a half hours, with the last fifteen minutes traversed through inner city congestion.

The vehicle felt like it had been crawling for kilometres when it darted right and then down what might've been a ramp. After circling sharply it came to a stop and she heard heavy footsteps approach the driver's side window.

A deep voice commanded, 'Pango wants her upstairs in his office.'

Moments later, still with her wrists bound behind her back and the hood over her head, she was lifted onto a familiar broad shoulder. On the plus side she wasn't leaning on a corpse any more, but on the downside, she was still captive.

Multiple footsteps echoed in what she suspected to be a subterranean car park, then she heard the ping of an elevator. As Boof stepped into the lift and turned to face outward, Modeen gasped as her head banged against two of the walls.

'Careful!' a voice growled. It was the man with the silver buckle.

'Sorry boss.'

'We've lugged her over two thousand kilometres, don't break her now, Boof.'

When the elevator doors swished open the men stepped out, turned left, and walked twenty paces down a corridor, their footsteps echoing off the hard wall and floor surfaces. Doors opened and closed and then their footsteps grew muffled as they crossed a section of carpet.

The man with the silver buckle ordered, 'There,' and Modeen felt Boof lean forward to set her on her feet. Then he pushed her against something narrow, cold and unyielding, and bound her to it.

A voice she didn't recognise barked, 'Strap her legs too.' After Boof hastened to comply, the voice commanded, 'Now remove her hood.'

As the pillowslip was tugged off her head, Modeen blinked and squinted. When her vision cleared it was to see cold blue eyes staring into hers. Tribal tattoos covered one side of the man's dark face, and when he spoke she glimpsed the inside of his lips and mouth. They were stained black.

'So we finally get to meet in person.' His matted dreadlocks danced as he tilted his head back and laughed. 'Cat got your tongue?' His eyes narrowed, his sneer vanished and he said stonily, 'It appears you don't remember me.' When she made no reply, he went on more pleasantly, 'I am the Nakahi Pango.' He gave a mocking bow. 'The Black Mamba.' Straightening, he ran his freakishly blue eyes over her face. 'And you were wearing a balaclava the last time I saw you.' He stepped back to look her up and down. 'I'm impressed. Quite the Marta Hari aren't you, both beautiful and dangerous.'

She held his gaze and kept her voice even. 'What do you want?'

'What do I want?' He grinned, revealing more of his ugly, stained mouth. 'Firstly, make no mistake, I always *get* what I want.' He tilted his chin to gaze at her thoughtfully. 'At first I wanted you dead ... but that was before I was informed of the bounty on your pretty head.' He moved closer and ran the back of a hand down the side of her face. When he tapped a long black finger-nail, curved and sharpened to a claw-like point, against the creamy skin of her cheek, she twisted her face away.

He gave another bark of mocking laughter. 'What's wrong, princess? Don't like to be touched? I'd get used to it if I were you, considering what's ahead for you.' Still smirking, he sauntered to an expansive glass-topped desk and bent to collect something. Turning to her again, he held up a photo. 'Although the other members of your unit have something quite different in their … short term … futures.'

When she realised the photo in his hand featured a uniformed Ben receiving his VC, she frowned.

'Oh, didn't I tell you?' Pango sneered, clearly enjoying himself. 'The bounty I mentioned earlier extends to them as well.'

She turned her head to sweep a glance around the room, noting the metal pole she was tied to. It was of the pole-dancing kind.

Naturally.

Then she saw the other items spread across the desk, a number of eight-by-ten photographs and beside them, her wallet.

'Ben Logan,' Pango went on smoothly. 'VC and leader of your unit.' He flicked the photo onto the desk and picked up two more, holding them out for her to see. 'Colleagues of yours?'

She recognised the images of Bugs and Spooky, cropped from one of their old Army photographs. Then he held up a picture of Wolf and her stomach did a back-flip.

His voice grew even more oily. 'Pity about this one, we won't be able to collect on him. He's in too many bits.'

It took a force of will for Modeen to keep her face expressionless, her gaze level, unblinking.

He's fishing, she told herself harshly. *Those photos are readily available online, and he doesn't know Wolf survived the explosion.*

'But you, Josephine Dakota Modeen, are a different story altogether,' Pango continued in that same slick tone. 'While they're only interested in seeing your team mates' heads separated from their bodies, my clients want you alive, and they're willing to pay substantially more for that privilege.' He threw a hand in the air, and the overhead light glinted off an enormous gold skull ring on one finger.

'You know how these middle eastern radicals think,' he went on as though chatting to an old friend. 'Everything has to be symbolic. So you're going to be a plaything, a curio if you will, to help their troops and suicide bombers feel better about themselves.' His eyes glinted and his blackened lips twisted into a sneer, and then he lifted his chin at a weedy little man standing in the corner.

The man approached her holding what looked to Modeen like a Geiger Counter. As he waved its paddle over her body and took particular care scanning her arms, the instrument produced a steady hum. After a minute he muttered, 'No bugs, no trackers. She's clean.'

'Well that's disappointing,' Pango said with a smirk. 'I was certain you'd lead them to us. Never mind, I'm sure the ASIO agent you were briefly acquainted with pointed them in the right direction before his sad demise.'

'You've got me,' Modeen said through tight lips, 'you don't need the others.'

He turned his head to look at her sideways. 'Is that right, Josephine?' Taking one long stride toward her, he thrust his face close to hers again. Even his breath was dark, foul and chilling. 'But they're the icing on the cake,' he murmured in her ear, 'and a cake without icing just won't do.'

She willed herself to stare straight ahead. 'If you're smart you'll quit while you're ahead. If they decide to come for me, they'll bring an army.'

'That's not how they operate though, is it?' He backed up a fraction, still smirking. 'And you're not Army any more, are you? You're something else, something covert.' As he spoke he fixed her with cold, contemptuous eyes. 'Covert … but not very clever, I'm afraid. Whatever you and your friends are, you certainly upset the wrong people on your most recent trip to Afghanistan.'

Turning away with a dismissive sniff, he barked at the man with the silver buckle, 'Take her to the lock-up, and post extra guards as we discussed.'

She felt someone come up behind her and then the pillowslip was pulled over her head again. Boof then proceeded to untie her from the pole and with a hand gripping her firmly under one arm, he led her away. When he stopped and let her go, she heard him back away as a heavy metal door clanged closed, followed by the decisive clunk of a lock being driven home. Reaching a beefy arm through the bars, Boof pulled her toward him and used the allen key to remove the shackles from her wrists.

With her hands now free, she reefed the hood from her head and dropped it to the floor. Rubbing the welts on her wrists, she looked around the three-by-two metre holding cell. It was decked out like a jail, with a single bunk in one corner and in the other, a plumbed-in toilet and grimy, dripping sink. There was no window and the air smelled stale, fetid. From the front corner to the right of the cell door, the green blink of an LED caught her eye. It was mounted next to the lens of a security camera.

Boof stood watching as she moved to perch herself on the edge of the bunk, leaning her elbows on her knees and cupping her head in her hands. Then, with a look she might've called contrite if she hadn't known better, he turned and was gone.

She sat contemplating what Nakahi Pango had told her.

He's using me to lure the others. Why is he confident they'll come? And he's so cocky … what makes him so sure he'll be able to overpower them?

Peeking through her fingers and finding no one looking her way, she ran a careful hand down her leg and felt around the top lining inside her boot. Relieved when her fingers brushed against the trusty electrode, she rose and walked nonchalantly around the cell, stopping at the door. She was about to grab one of the bars when her radar kicked in. She paused before cautiously tapping the metal with the back of her hand and…

CRACK!

Electricity arced blue between the bar and her fingers. Her hand flew back as the muscles in her arm contracted and she sucked in an irate breath.

Great! That was just what I needed after those Taserings.

She rolled her shoulder and gave her arm a vigorous rub as the guard stationed a few feet down the corridor sniggered, 'That's right, it's electrified.'

After glancing down the hallway in both directions, taking care not to get too close to the bars again, Modeen turned and resumed her seat on the bunk.

CHAPTER NINETEEN

The five storey building sat squarely on the corner of Mercury Lane and Karangahape Road in Auckland's central business district. It had undergone several face-lifts since its construction in the 1930s, but retained its art deco style. Using the mouse to rotate the 3D thermal image of the structure on his laptop, Ben noted that the ground floor with its rows of boutique shops was the least occupied.

Most of the human heat signatures were located on the fourth level and in the fifth floor penthouse, which was recessed well back into the centre of the structure's flat roof. They were big signatures ... except for a slender, more shapely one in a central room of the penthouse.

Ben zoomed in on the womanly figure. Lying prone, it was surrounded by multiple signatures dotted throughout that level. His eyes narrowed and he flicked a glance at the wall clock in NatSec's briefing room. Reaching for the phone, he dialled an extension number. 'Leanne, how soon can you get me on a flight to Auckland, New Zealand?'

'I'll just check.' He heard hear tapping on a keyboard and then she announced, 'Next available flight leaves Tullamarine in ninety minutes.'

'Book me on it.'

'I'll email you the e-ticket.'

'Thanks.' Ben hung up and then dialled another number. The instant it was answered he barked, 'Sit rep, Bugs.'

'We're about an hour away from the docks. Should have an update for you then.'

'Belay that order. I want you to stake out a building in Auckland's CBD, at the corner of …,' Ben paused. 'You got a pen?'

'Yep.'

'Karangahape Road and Mercury Lane. That's K A R A N G A H A P E Road, got it?'

'Got it.'

'Keep a low profile. Unless absolutely necessary, don't engage anyone. I'm flying in, so pick me up from the airport six hours from now. You got any spare kit?'

'Yep, this Humvee's fully loaded.' There was a grin in Bugs' voice when he added, 'Glad you're joinin' the action. With Wolf out of the picture we could use a good door-kicker.'

With a mildly amused, 'Humph,' followed by, 'see you in six,' Ben signed off.

———

Wolf's dark head was visible above the string of passengers making their way into Auckland airport's arrivals lounge. While he moved freely enough, duffel slung over one broad shoulder, to Salty's keen eyes the young man had lost weight and was missing the athletic spring in his step. His focused expression was etched with worry lines, due more to Modeen's situation than his own, Salty surmised.

He made his way toward Wolf through the waiting throng. 'Hey there, youngster.'

Stopping in his tracks, Wolf frowned. 'Salty?' He stared at the other man for a second and then raised a sardonic eyebrow. 'I guess it's no coincidence I've bumped into you here.'

Salty threw him a wink. 'Ben thought you might need a hand.'

'I bet he did.' Wolf's half grin faded and he was all business again. 'Have you had an update from him? I haven't been able to reach him, he must have his phone off or be out of range.'

'According to Bugs, Ben's in transit which'll be why you can't get him. He's arriving in Auckland within the hour.'

'Good.' Wolf gave a brisk nod. 'If Ben's coming it's a

safe bet that Jo's still alive, and we haven't missed the main event.'

'That's exactly what I was thinking.' Salty thumped Wolf's firm, well-muscled shoulder with a fist. 'We might make a decent agent out of you yet.' At Wolf's amused grunt, he went on. 'The guys are staking out a building in the CBD so I've booked us into a hotel close by. We'll go there and check in soon as you've collected your baggage.'

'Nothin' to collect, only brought carry-on. I'm good to go.' Wolf was already moving toward the exit.

Salty gave a wry snort. The youngster was keen to get moving, and with good cause. 'Right-o then, let's head.'

The taxi pulled in down a lane off Pitts Street, in between the Chatman Hotel and a Methodist Church. Looking up at the cross mounted on the roof of the church, Salty quipped, 'A good sign. We need all the help we can get.' He glanced across at Wolf, who merely grunted and continued staring ahead. To Salty's eyes, the young man's whole body was wound tight as though poised for action.

Smart of Ben to keep him on the sidelines, Salty mused. *Too far from the action and he'd be like a caged tiger liable to break out at any time. Too close and he'd be a loaded pistol likely to go off. And considering the stakes, who could blame him?*

As the taxi slowed at the rear of the hotel, Wolf had

his door open before the cab stopped rolling. Salty paid the driver while Wolf collected their bags from the boot, and then both men strode into reception.

When an attractive young woman glanced up at them from the desk, Salty said pleasantly, 'Hello young lady.'

She returned his smile. 'Hello.' Running her almond-shaped eyes over the cheery older man and his silent, rather grim-looking companion, she noted the younger man's muscular physique and wondered idly if he were the older gent's bodyguard. 'You both checking in?'

'Yeah, bookings under Ryan and Salt.' As she turned to check her computer screen, Salty asked, 'Do you have any rooms available on the top floor, in this front corner if possible?'

The receptionist flicked him a glance. 'The front corner?' At his nod, she looked back at the screen. 'We've got a couple of corner rooms available, but only one on the eighth floor. The other is on the fifth.'

'Perfect. The youngster here will take the one on the fifth and I'll take the eighth.'

She looked at him enquiringly. 'You don't mind being on different floors?'

'Nope.'

She proceeded with the booking and handed them their room keys, wishing them a pleasant stay. Salty thanked her and joined Wolf outside the elevator.

When they stepped into the lift and Salty pressed the button for the fifth floor, Wolf threw him a questioning glance. 'Higher is better so shouldn't we go straight to the eighth?'

Salty waited for the door to close completely before answering. 'We'll see what the vantage point is like on the fifth. At least with two levels at our disposal we've got a couple of options.'

After grunting his agreement, Wolf stood silently engrossed in his thoughts as the lift carried them upward. When the door swished open he strode out with Salty close behind. Letting them into the apartment, he dropped his duffel on the floor and tossed the key on the table on his way to the side window.

Salty paused to take a folder out of his bag and then put it on the table, opening it to reveal an eight-by-ten photo of Owen Patel and two other Maori men. He tapped a finger on the photo and called to Wolf, 'This is the main person of interest, and a couple of his known associates.'

At Wolf's glance around and nod of acknowledgement, Salty joined him at the window and pointed across the roof of the church toward an art deco building on Karangahape Road. 'That's the building we're staking out, there.' He bent to take a pair of binoculars from his bag. 'Looks like this level gives us a better view of the top floor and penthouse.' Passing the binoculars to Wolf he said, 'Keep an eye out. I'll go to my room, dump my stuff, and then duck out and get us some supplies.'

Putting the binoculars to his eyes, Wolf focused them on the beige-coloured building. The late afternoon sun reflected brightly off the large banks of windows on its top three floors and penthouse, making it difficult to define the blurred silhouettes moving about inside.

Hearing the door close behind Salty, Wolf lowered the binoculars. Taking out the mobile phone Ben had given him, he dialled a number from memory.

His call was answered promptly, with a jaunty, 'Yeah?'

'Bugs?'

'Wolfman! How are'ya buddy?'

'I'm here, at the Chatman Hotel on Pitts Street. Come get me, will ya?'

After a short pause Bugs said with a hint of regret in his voice, 'Sorry buddy, no can do. Spook 'n I are on a stakeout, and then one of us is pickin' up the big guy when he flies in.'

Wolf gave a peeved exhalation. 'Come on, Bugs, this is Modeen we're talkin' about. You can't leave me stuck here with a pair of binoculars and a crusty old man.'

'Hey, I get how you must be feelin' mate, but we got our orders. Ben's leadin' this gig and wants us to wait, so sit tight and we'll keep you in the loop. Besides, you shouldn't underestimate Salty, he might surprise ya. Anyway, I gotta go, mate.'

'But—' Hearing Bugs ring off Wolf gave a frustrated roar and lobbed the phone onto the sofa, making it bounce a few times before coming to rest. After pacing up and down in front of the window, he flopped onto the edge of the sofa and put his head in his hands.

Was Jo now mere metres away from him, in the building just up the street?

Balling his hands into fists, he thumped them into the sofa's soft seat.

He HAD to get to her. She needed him, of that he was convinced.

His insides were in turmoil. His heart said go, Go, GO! but his head and the soldier in him said wait. He was unarmed and had no idea what he'd be up against. At that moment, the old army saying, *hurry up and wait,* took on a whole new meaning.

He was still battling with himself when Salty returned, wearing a backpack and carrying two bass guitar cases.

As he set down the cases Salty eyed him with concern. 'You OK, youngster?' Shrugging off the backpack, he placed it on the table.

Wolf didn't look up. 'I just feel so *useless,*' he muttered darkly.

Salty stared at him for a long moment and then opened the backpack. When he called, 'Heads up,' Wolf glanced over and he tossed him a foot-long ham and salad roll in a wrapper. 'It ain't chowder,' Salty chirped, 'but it should take the edge off.'

Catching the roll with one hand, Wolf dropped it on the sofa beside him, mumbling, 'Thanks, but a rifle would've been more use.' He put the binoculars to his eyes again and stared across at the building.

Behind him, Salty grinned as he lifted one of the

guitar cases onto the table. Clicking it open, he removed a semi-automatic rifle, pulled the slide back and released it.

Wolf's ears pricked at the sound and his head snapped around. On seeing the weapon in Salty's hands, he said excitedly, 'Is that an R2?'

Salty shrugged. 'My contact says it goes bang, and that it's got the latest long range thermal scope, bipod and suppressor. You can go single shot or semi-auto.'

Wolf strode to his side and took the rifle from him. Running his eyes over it, he said, 'You've done good, mate.' He dropped the magazine and thumbed out one of the bullets, murmuring, 'Seven-point-six-two.' He nodded. 'Yep, you've done really good.' Pointing the weapon at the building, he adjusted the high tech scope.

'There's more.' Salty lifted the next guitar case onto the table, clicked the latches and flipped it open. The weapon nestled in the cut-out foam was in military camouflage colours.

Setting the R2 down on the sofa, Wolf picked up the second rifle, pulled out the magazine, and shook his head.

Salty frowned. 'What's wrong?'

'This is a US Cheytac M200 Intervention point four-o-eight.'

'Yeah, so?'

'So it's a beautiful weapon ... with an effective range of *over* two kilometres.' Wolf lifted his stubbled chin toward the art deco building. 'Our target is just over two hundred metres away, making this canon seriously over the top for the job. Even if I hit the target, the bullet would likely go straight through and out the other side of the building.'

'OK then.' Salty reached for the rifle. 'I'll put it away.'

'Hell no!' Wolf kept a firm hold of the weapon, extending its retractable stock. 'Set 'er up. Y'never know, it could come in handy. We might need to stop an elephant.'

'Right. So, what else do you need?'

'That,' and Wolf indicated the writing desk tucked into a corner of the room.

Salty picked it up. 'Where do you want it?'

'Here, by the window.' When Salty had the desk in position, Wolf set up the Remington R2 on it. Straightening, he ran his fingers over the window glass. 'Got a hammer in that bag of tricks of yours?'

Salty reached into his backpack and came out with a suction cup and a metal rod fitted with a diamond cutting tip. 'How big a hole do you want?'

With a throaty laugh, Wolf pulled the table back from the window saying, 'One-fifty radius, thanks.'

Seeing his wry head shake, Salty barked, 'What?'

'Bugs said I shouldn't underestimate you.' Wolf threw him a rueful half grin. 'And he was right on the money.'

———

Ben strode past the taxi rank outside the main entrance of Auckland's international airport. He had exchanged his usual suit and business shoes for black cargos and a pair of combat boots. His hulking biceps rippled under the sleeves of a khaki T-shirt as he shaded his eyes, on the look-out for his ride. A short time later a desert camouflage Humvee came into view, its width dominating one side of the dual-lane road. With a soft squeal of fat, all-terrain tyres it lumbered to a halt, taking up one and a bit parking bays to the annoyance of nearby motorists.

When Ben jumped into the front passenger's side, Bugs reported without preamble, 'We've set up base on East Street as you requested. Spooky's stakin' out the building. No unusual activity so far.'

'Wolf and Salty?'

'They've received their package and are in position.'

'Good.' Ben gave a brisk nod as Bugs accelerated away from the pick-up area. 'That should keep Wolf occupied for the time being.'

CHAPTER TWENTY

On Karangahape Road in the CBD, in a concealed section of the basement of the art deco building, cold blue eyes scanned multiple banks of LED screens displaying images streamed from cameras positioned in the building's penthouse and fourth floor. A wicked grin spread across the man's face revealing black-stained lips and mouth, and when he jerked his head at another man standing nearby, his dreadlocks jiggled greasily.

'Get going,' he barked, 'it's time to bait the hook. And tell the others to take up positions.' He threw the man a sharp glance. 'And remind them to stay alert.'

About to comply, the man paused to frown over his shoulder. 'You sure we've got enough men?'

His boss gave a derisive snort. 'These fools work in small teams, so yes, we have more than enough men to handle them.'

· · ·

Modeen was lying on the bunk, hands behind her head, when the man with the silver buckle came to her cell door. He rapped on the wrought iron bars with a be-ringed hand and barked, 'Hood on, hands through the bars. We're going for a walk.' When she didn't budge he reached down to pointedly finger the Taser lodged in his waistband.

With a roll of eyes, she sat up and began pulling on her boots.

The man exhaled loudly and then snarled, 'Today!'

She bent to scoop up the black pillowslip from the floor where she'd dropped it earlier, saying sweetly, 'What's the hurry?'

He responded by banging the bars again and growling, 'Move.'

With a nonchalant lift of one eyebrow Modeen stepped closer, pulling the pillowslip over her head and then threading both hands through the gap between two bars.

The man snapped the shackles on her wrists and then opened the door. 'Secure her legs.'

'Yes boss.'

She recognised Boof's voice, amid the clattering of chains as shackles were bolted to her ankles. He moved with purpose, connecting another chain from her ankles to the shackles on her wrists in convict-style fashion. Trussed like that, she was unable to raise her arms above her waist. When she felt a meaty hand – Boof's no doubt – grasp her arm and urge her on, she began shuffling forward. Her ears pricked at the sound of another set of shackles rattling past in the corridor, and then the door to her cell slammed shut behind her.

'Keep moving!' It was the man with the silver buckle. As he spoke, he shoved her in the back, making her stumble forward.

———

'Spooky still in place?' Ben was opening his laptop and didn't look at Bugs.

'Yep, he's on the stakeout, in the carpark opposite the building.' Braking outside an aged timber cottage sandwiched between industrial sheds on East Street, Bugs eyed the garage beside the house. Muttering, 'Don't breathe in,' he carefully reversed the wide vehicle through the garage's narrow entrance. It scraped past with mere millimetres to spare on either side. Fortunately the structure's interior was wide enough to allow them to open their doors.

While Bugs was manoeuvring the Humvee, Ben dialled a number and put the mobile to his ear. 'Spook, return to base.'

Fifteen minutes later Spooky joined the two men in the cottage's kitchen. He eyed the shabby sixties-style green laminate table on rust-pitted chrome legs. It was strewn with tactical gear, thermal night vision goggles, C4 charges, sleeping agent canisters, stun grenades, pistols and ammunition.

Ben greeted him with a nod and turned his laptop so they could all see the screen. Bringing up a thermal image of the building, he zoomed in to a small room in the centre of the penthouse and what appeared to be a female figure lying on a bunk in the corner. At his curt, 'I believe this is where they're holding JD,' the other two nodded. Then he fixed Spooky with a narrow-eyed, pensive gaze. 'How many guards in the adjoining carpark?'

'Two on the roof and one on the gantry level in the building opposite.'

'We'll wait until o-one hundred. Hopefully by that time there'll be less civilians in the vicinity.' When Ben added brusquely, 'Right, listen up,' Bugs and Spooky leaned in, focusing their full attention on him as he brought up images of Owen Patel and his known goons, and then outlined their plan of attack.

———

At o-one hundred, Auckland's CBD was quiet save for the odd taxi ferrying heavy-eyed travellers or party animals to their various destinations. It was a dark, chilly night, and the street lights cast a hazy glow in the gathering mist. The three fit-looking men strolled down East Street, duffels slung over their shoulders. Every now and then one of them would say something and all three would laugh, projecting late night nonchalance, but a keen-eyed observer may have picked up the air of purpose beneath their charade.

They followed the road south as it curved and connected with Upper Queen Street, then they turned left onto Cross Road, which ran behind the art deco building on Karangahape Road.

Keeping his gaze forward and his voice low, Spooky said, 'Up there on the right is our target,' and he indicated the art deco building with a lift of his chin. 'The third gantry connects the rear of the building to the multi-level carpark across the road to our left. I've disabled the cameras in the carpark.'

After taking a quick glance at the target, Ben muttered, 'Good work,' adding, 'we're lucky it's a dark night.'

They entered the carpark through the street-level entrance and climbed the stairs to the fourth level. They moved silently in single file, with Spooky as point man leading them around the parking bays until they were situated just above the third gantry. Slinging their duffels onto their backs, they scaled the safety railing and then dropped onto the roof of the gantry, taking care to keep the noise to a minimum.

Away from the street lighting darkness closed in. As one, the three paused to don night vision goggles, webbing and weapons. Ben switched his goggles to thermal imaging, and carrying a Lewis CQB16 assault rifle, he moved across the roof of the six metre long gantry, keeping as low as his six foot four frame would allow. Squatting on his haunches at the other end of the gantry, he turned and surveyed the roof of the carpark. After the nearest guard moved away, oblivious to their presence, Ben motioned for the others to follow.

Bugs crossed next. As he drew near, Ben cupped his hands and bent to take Bug's leading foot to boost him onto the roof of the connecting building. He did the same for Spooky, and then shimmied up the external air conditioning duct to join them. For a big man, he moved with an athletic grace that indicated a high level of fitness.

From there they vaulted onto the next roof level, where Bugs jimmied the lock on an external service door. Entering the art deco building through a utility room on level three, they made their way past abandoned offices, moving silently in the eerie stillness.

At Ben's hand signal, Spooky peeled off to set a C4 charge at the main power sub-board.

The other two went on to the stairwell, where Ben pressed a finger to his ear comms piece. 'Wolf, you copy?'

The gruff reply was almost instant. 'Copy.'

'Stand-by, we're about to kill the lights.'

'Affirmative. Switching to thermal imaging.' On the fifth floor of the Chatman Hotel, Wolf turned to Salty who was sitting by his side in the darkness, looking through a tripod mounted scope. 'The show's about to start.'

Salty lifted his head a fraction. 'You ready to rock and roll, youngster?'

'Ready.'

Thirty seconds later the C4 detonated, blowing the door clean off the sub-board and cutting the power to the upper floors of the art deco building. After a short pause Wolf announced over the comms, 'Confirm lights out on top levels. I see four hostiles north end of the fourth level, six in the penthouse. All armed with assault rifles. They're wearing night vision goggles, and are covering the elevator and stairs.'

Thinking, *there goes our advantage,* Ben rubbed his chin thoughtfully and then turned to Bugs. 'Go stand by the elevator, wait for my signal then send the lift to the penthouse.' As he spoke, he unhooked a stun grenade from Bugs' webbing and handed it to him.

Bugs frowned. 'But didn't we just kill the power?'

Spooky answered him. 'Elevator's on a different circuit.'

'Oh, right.'

Ben thumped Bugs on the shoulder. 'Wait for my signal,' then, 'Spook, you're with me.' With Spooky by his side, Ben pulled open the door to the stairwell and charged through, startling a guard stationed there.

The man was turning to level his M4 Carbine at the intruders when Ben's size twelve combat boot stomped him square in the midsection, sending him back against the concrete wall. As he rebounded, his skull was snapped backward by a powerful elbow to the forehead. He slumped to the ground, to lie motionless as the two men raced up the stairwell. They went past level four and stopped at the door leading to the penthouse.

When Ben turned to him holding the canister of sleeping agent and the half-face respirator he'd taken from his webbing, Spooky nodded and unclipped his own gear.

Ben whispered, 'Now, Bugs,' into his comms.

Two levels below them, Bugs pressed the call button for the elevator. When it arrived he leaned in, hit the number for the top floor, and then stepped back, pulling the pin on the stun grenade in his hand. As the doors swished closed he lobbed the grenade onto the floor of the lift before turning and racing up the stairwell to join the others, taking the steps two at a time.

Wolf's voice came over the comms. 'Movement on both floors. They're all headin' for the elevator.'

In the front room of the penthouse, all six guards gathered around the lift, lined up shoulder to shoulder, weapons levelled at the elevator doors. As the lift opened they let loose a hail of bullets, only stopping when they realised there was no return fire. As the air cleared they stared blankly into the empty elevator, and then one of them opened his mouth to shout a warning—

BOOM!

They staggered back from the blinding flash and deafening explosion, gasping and shielding their heads with their arms. They didn't see Ben and Spooky leap from the stairwell, pull the pins on their sleeping agent canisters and roll them into the group. As the six guards dropped to the floor, Bugs hastily fitted his respirator and then joined Ben and Spooky as they made for the corridor leading to the central rooms.

When Ben turned the corner, he ran head-on into a guard coming up the corridor armed with an M4. Deflecting the guard's weapon, he drove the barrel of his rifle deep into the man's chest and squeezed the trigger. He pushed the sagging body aside and carried on, only stopping at the barred door of the central cell. Through the darkness his night vision goggles projected the thermal image of a woman lying on the bunk bed, her head hooded and her ankles and wrists bound.

While Bugs continued down the corridor, scouting for more guards, Ben gave the barred door a shake and hissed, 'JD! JD, get up!' The door rattled but wouldn't budge, and neither did the woman. Muttering, 'They must've drugged her,' he turned to Spooky standing at his side, and tapped a finger on the door lock.

Pulling another C4 charge from inside his combat vest, Spooky fixed it to the cell door's locking mechanism and set the timer. Yelling, 'Fire in the hole, Modeen,' he and Ben stepped back and turned their faces away, covering their ears.

A second later a blast shattered the lock, sending shards of metal into the air and splintering to the floor. Not waiting for the dust to settle, Ben raced into the cell and kneeled beside the bunk. Grabbing her by the arms, he urged, 'JD, wake up.' When she didn't respond he pulled the hood from her head and stared down at her, frowning at the fresh track marks on her inner arms.

Hearing Bugs fire a short burst just down the corridor from them, Spooky yelled, 'Let's go!'

'It's … it's not her.' Ben still held the woman by the arms. She blinked one languid eye at him before falling back into her drugged stupor.

Right at that moment a guard ran diagonally across the head of the corridor and dove forward to punch the panic button mounted on the wall. Instantly two iron-barred gates dropped from the ceiling at either end of the corridor, as Spooky let off a burst from his assault rifle and neutralised the guard.

'Bugs!'

At Spooky's shout, Bugs appeared at the other end of the corridor and propped just outside the iron gate.

'On the wall, the button!' Spooky yelled. 'Behind you!'

Turning, Bugs scanned the wall and then punched the button. With a metallic groan both gates slowly rose into the ceiling again.

'This way!' Bugs called. 'There's a back door.'

'Ben!' Spooky yelled, 'We need to *go!*'

Staring down at the woman, Ben frowned and muttered, 'Can't just leave her here,' and gathered her into his arms.

In the Chatman Salty said urgently, 'The guards have left the fourth floor and are heading up the stairwell.'

Focusing his sights on the stairwell door leading into

the penthouse, Wolf announced over the comms, 'Another four hostiles comin' your way.'

Ben's voice crackled back at him. 'Hold 'em off. We gotta find another way out.'

When the stairwell door opened and the first of the guards tentatively peered into the room, a bullet shattered the large section of glass at the front of the penthouse and tore the night vision goggles off the top of the guard's head. The man instantly retreated to the safety of the stairwell.

Salty glanced at Wolf. 'Did you mean to do that?'

'Just sendin' them a message.'

Salty grinned. 'Well in that case, nice shot.'

Wolf kept the cross-hairs of his scope fixed on the door. When another guard sprang from the stairwell and tried to race across the room for cover, Wolf dropped him with a bullet to the temple before he could get a metre from the doorway. Following up with another five rounds in quick succession, Wolf put the bullets into the door at head height, neatly grouped together in a one inch diameter circle.

Keeping the R2 trained on the door, he drawled, 'They should get the message now.'

On McKinnon Drive, the black Ford Transit slowed when the passenger noticed flashes of rifle fire coming from the Chatman Hotel. Shouting, 'Pull up here!' the man with the silver buckle tugged a high-powered hunting rifle from behind the front seats.

Boof stayed at the wheel while his boss leapt from the vehicle. Sliding the cargo door open, the man with the silver buckle jumped inside, straightaway turning to face outward. Behind him, Modeen cocked her head, listening intently, and then soundlessly scrunched herself into a ball. This enabled her to grasp the top of her hood, and when she straightened, the pillowslip slid from her head.

She blinked, taking in the man in front of her. He was using the side of the van's door frame to steady a hunting rifle. As he took aim, she followed the line of the gun's barrel to the fifth level of a hotel across the freeway from their position. He paused, waiting for the van to stop rocking in the wake of a passing truck, and then—

Lunging forward, Modeen threw her shackled arms over his head and then thrust herself backward, burying the chain linking the shackles deep into his throat. He gave a strangled gasp and dropped the rifle as blood rushed to his face, engorging a vein in his temple. He flailed his arms, struggling for air as Modeen increased the pressure on his windpipe. She made to wrap her legs around his body and thereby gain more leverage, but the shackles on her ankles hampered her movements.

In desperation, the man jerked an elbow into her, sending her against the wall of the van. His head slid free and he clutched at his throat, sucking in air. A split second later Modeen rebounded, landing an elbow to the side of his face. When she fell forward, sliding down his chest, she caught a glimpse of the hated Taser tucked into the front of his pants. Jamming a finger on the trigger, she held it there and watched him jerk when the electrodes speared into his flesh, an instant before his body began convulsing violently.

She felt the van rock as Boof exited the driver's side to come to his boss's aid. He appeared in front of the cargo hold and abruptly froze. Modeen had grabbed the Glock from the back of silver buckles' waistband and was holding it trained at Boof's head.

She said quietly, 'Don't make me shoot you, Boof.' When he hesitated, she snapped, 'Run, *now*, before I change my mind.'

He stared at her for a second, wide-eyed and uncertain, before raising his hands and backing away. Then his heavy tread faded into the distance, and he was gone.

Lowering the pistol to her side, she turned her attention to the man with the silver buckle. His body had stopped convulsing but his face was still contorted with pain. She gave a derisive snort and reached for the Taser again. He twitched his head, pleading with his eyes, but she merely smiled and pressed the trigger again.

'That's twice,' she said, holding it on for a few more seconds. 'Now we're even.' After releasing the trigger, she began rifling through his pants pockets. Finding the allen key, she promptly unlocked her ankle shackles. Dropping them to the floor, she began working on her wrists. They proved more problematic to open, and while she was occupied, his body stopped convulsing. Her hands were still bound when he made a surprise lunge for the Glock. She intercepted his hands as he grabbed hold of the gun and bashed his knuckles against the floor of the van to make him release the weapon. When that didn't work, she spun around and pinned his gun hand under one knee before driving the point of her elbow hard into his throat.

His whole body jerked in response and he threw up his free hand to smack her in the side of the face with a clenched fist. The force of the blow sent her to the floor. Rebounding once more, she deflected his gun arm across her body as he let loose two shots. They sailed harmlessly through the roof of the van.

Straddling his body, she used all her weight to turn the weapon back on him and then…

Crack, crack!

Two more shots rang out.

Rolling off him, Modeen slumped to the floor of the van.

CHAPTER TWENTY-ONE

Bugs held the door open for Spooky to lead the way down a narrow flight of stairs at the back of the penthouse. Once everyone had passed through, Bugs made sure they weren't being tailed before closing the door and following them. With Ben still carrying the anonymous woman, the three of them exited the stairwell on the fourth floor, where they moved swiftly and quietly along a corridor toward another flight of wider stairs.

They continued making their way downward with Spooky leading, Ben following, and Bugs covering the rear.

In the building's basement, the man watching the camera feeds swore loudly and sprang to his feet.

. . .

Stopping abruptly as he passed the first floor landing, Spooky beat a hasty retreat, signalling to the others to get out of the stairwell. They dashed onto the first floor level, and just as Spooky closed the door behind them an explosion erupted at the base of the stairs, shaking the whole building. Ben hunched over the woman in his arms, his broad back taking the brunt of the explosive force as the stairwell door burst from its hinges. As all four were sent crashing to the floor amid the debris and dust, Ben tightened his grip on the woman and twisted in mid-air to land on his back, protecting her from injury.

Bugs was the first to his feet. He dusted himself off, shaking bits of plaster from his buzz-cut hair, and then gave Ben a hand up. After a quick examination of the twisted mess of metal hand rails and concrete in the stairwell, he looked over at Spooky, who was up and dusting himself off, and called, 'We can't get out that way.' Lifting his chin, Bugs indicated the settling dust at the other end of the hallway. 'Looks like they blew both exits.'

Hearing that, Ben moved to an office on the right of the corridor and kicked in the door. As he strode into the room he spied an office chair shoved into a corner. It appeared to be in reasonable condition, so he carefully lowered the woman into it. After making sure she was secure, he left her to walk to the window. Flicking up his night vision goggles he peered outside to get his bearings.

One flight below their position, the ground floor

lights illuminated the nearest section of Cross Road. When he glanced to the side he saw the gantry they'd traversed nearby. Looking right toward the intersection of Cross Road and Mercury Lane, he noticed a black limousine cruise past at a leisurely speed.

And through the open rear window he glimpsed Owen Patel in the back seat.

Putting a finger to his earpiece he barked, 'Wolf! The black Chrysler 300 limo heading your way, take out the driver.'

In the Chatman, Wolf pressed his forehead against the window and frowned. 'Negative Ben, I can't see the road from here.' Jumping up, he raced to the front quarter window, just as the limousine cruised past the building. 'Wait! I see it.'

'Take it out.'

Seeing Wolf scoop up the Cheytac as he rushed to the door, Salty quipped, 'You seen an elephant?' while gathering his tripod scope and hurrying after him.

Wolf took the stairs. Cursing the slower than normal response of his recuperating limbs, he used the handrails on one side as leverage to power up to the top floor. Finding the door to the roof locked, he bunched up and tried to kick it open. Built to withstand fire, the solid barricade didn't budge.

Swearing under his breath, he levelled the Cheytac at the lock, loaded the first round into the breech, and was about to pull the trigger when Salty came up behind him and yelled, 'Wait!' Passing the tripod to Wolf, he whipped out a Glock fitted with a silencer, and aimed it at the lock.

Blat, blat! Blat!

Taking the tripod back, he said, 'Try that.'

This time when Wolf lent against the door it fell open, revealing the building's flat roof line. The two men ran to the Pitt Street edge and got there in time to see the limousine disappear from sight as it turned onto the freeway.

Salty leaned out, peering after it, and then whirled around to thump Wolf on the shoulder. 'It'll pop out over here!' He ran to the southern edge of the roof and promptly set up the tripod as Wolf jogged after him.

Dropping to the roof, Wolf set up the rifle on the edge and settled onto his stomach behind it, muttering, 'Find me a target, Salty.'

'Capital letter 'A' in the graffiti on the side of the overpass, three hundred metres.'

Wolf searched through the rifle scope and zeroed in on the graffiti. It read *All Blacks* in large, colourful letters. He took a breath, exhaled it slowly, and fired off a shot.

A second later Salty, peering through the tripod scope, reported, 'Pretty much dead-centre but about an inch high.'

'It's probably sighted-in at eight hundred,' Wolf muttered, 'but I can work with that.'

Silence returned to the roof as the two men waited, poised and ready for the next move. Then Salty pointed across the freeway. 'Crap! They've taken the south-east exit.' He turned his scope while Wolf adjusted his position.

The instant he was ready, Wolf barked, 'Call it.'

'Fourteen hundred metres.'

Locating the limousine through the rifle's scope, Wolf murmured, 'Keep callin' it,' as he followed the vehicle's progress, at the same time taking in the surroundings and the angle of the shot.

'Fourteen-fifty,' Salty called. 'Fifteen … fifteen-fifty.'

BOOM!

Picking up the woman again and throwing her over his shoulder, Ben waved the others forward and all three shimmied down the fire hose Bugs had unravelled from the wall and fed through the window.

Once down they crossed the road, and Ben was just lowering the woman to the ground by the wall of the carpark when another explosion erupted in the art deco building. The three men braced themselves as the ground shook beneath their feet and behind them the penthouse and fourth floor collapsed inward onto the third and then the second levels of the art deco building.

Through the settling dust the three jogged away from the scene.

As he ran Spooky took out his mobile. 'Should I call it in?'

'No, we need to get moving.' Ben lengthened his

stride. 'Someone would've heard that, so Emergency Services should be on their way.'

After the reverberation of the shot dispersed, Salty began, 'I think you miss—' but then saw the limousine veer left down the embankment, roll several times, and burst into flames.

With the rifle scope still trained on the vehicle, Wolf reported over the comms, 'Driver and vehicle neutralised, south eastern arterial freeway.'

Ben stopped to reply with a gruff, 'Acknowledged. We're heading back to get the Humvee.' He was about to move on when Wolf's voice came over the comms again, this time with a distinct thread of tension that was out of character for the big man.

'What about Jo?' He paused as though hating having to ask. 'Do you have her? Is she safe?'

His three mates stopped in their tracks and shared a pained glance, and then Ben spoke up with a hint of regret in his deep voice. 'I can't elaborate on that at the moment, Wolf. Stand by, I'll keep you posted.'

'Can't elaborate?' Wolf's frustration crackled over the comms. 'What does that mean? It's me you're talkin' to, Ben, so don't try to blow me off. Just tell me, was she there or wasn't she?'

With a resigned sigh, as though he'd anticipated this situation might arise, Ben said, 'Stand by, we'll swing past to pick you up,' and then switched off his comms unit. Seeing the other two looking at him with questions in their eyes, he merely shrugged and said, 'C'mon, let's go.'

Minutes later they were piling into the Humvee. As Bugs nosed the wide vehicle out of the garage Ben said crisply, 'We'll check out the limo first.'

After joining the freeway they headed south-east, and pulled up on the verge above the wrecked limousine. In the distance they could hear approaching sirens and glimpsed through the buildings the blue and red flashing lights of emergency vehicles rushing toward their position.

The limo was on its roof, still burning, with its boot, bonnet and two of the doors open. 'Quick Spook,' Ben ordered, 'check it out.'

'What about them?' Spooky indicated the noisily approaching convoy.

Ben waved him on. 'Go, I'll stall them.'

Leaping nimbly over the edge of the road, Spooky raced down to the smoking wreck, taking care to stay clear of the flames.

Bugs walked up to stand by Ben's side and murmured ominously, 'I hope she wasn't in there.'

Ben's lips were tight when he muttered, 'Me too,' just as the first ambulance arrived. Stepping forward, he flagged it down. When the nearest paramedic opened his window Ben said grimly, 'It's not safe to approach yet, it could blow at any minute. You'd better wait for Fire and Rescue to get here first and put out the flames.'

The paramedic stared at the wreck and nodded. 'They're on the way.'

When Ben's phone vibrated in his pocket, he clicked his tongue in annoyance. Pulling it out, he strode away to take the call. Not recognising the caller's number, he thought twice before answering. When he did, it was with a curt, 'Smith.' But his heart leapt into his mouth when a female voice said, 'Got a favour to ask Ben ... any chance you could arrange someone to come get me?'

His eyes widened and he said in a strangled voice, 'JD? Where ... where are you?'

'Pretty sure I'm in Auckland, New Zealand....'

'Where exactly in Auckland?'

He could tell she was looking around when she answered, 'I've just turned off ... Symonds Street into City Road and am parked opposite number seven, a high-rise office building.'

'Stay right there,' Ben ordered, 'I'll have someone pick you up in ten.' Ending the call, he sprinted back to the Humvee just as Spooky appeared at the top of the verge. Yelling, 'Get in, you can brief us on the way!' Ben jumped into the driver's seat, still issuing orders. 'Bugs, call Wolf and have him wait for us in front of the Chatman Hotel.'

The instant Spooky sprang into the back seat, the Humvee's tyres squealed as Ben gunned the vehicle.

'Wolf capped the driver,' Spooky said breathlessly, grabbing the front bucket seats to steady himself and leaning between them to deliver his report. 'But it wasn't Patel.'

Staring at the road ahead, Ben frowned. 'Patel was in the back seat.'

Spooky shook his head. 'No other bodies in the vehicle, just the driver.'

Ben powered through the gears, barking, 'Black Chrysler 300, stretch limo?' The six-point-five litre turbocharged V8 diesel roared as the Humvee gathered speed.

'Yep, with the driver's brains all over the dash, and no one in the back seat.'

'Any tracks?'

'I'll have to check later … didn't have much time before the firies arrived. Will stake it out after they've gone. Hopefully they won't make too much of a mess at the scene.'

With more squealing of all-terrain tyres, Ben turned off the freeway. 'Bugs, did you get onto Wolf?'

'Yeah he's waitin' for us.' Bugs fixed Ben with a curious gaze. 'What's goin' on?'

Saying enigmatically, 'You'll see,' Ben pulled the Humvee into Pitts Street and skidded to a stop in front of Wolf and Salty, standing waiting on the roadside.

When Bugs rolled down the passenger's side window, Salty smiled at him. 'Got room for me too?'

'Sure.' Bugs gave him a wide, toothy grin. 'We could fit four across the back seat of this bus.'

Thinking, *and we're gonna have to,* Ben waited just long enough for the two men to jump into the back before accelerating hard and cutting across to Queen Street. Ignoring Wolf's, 'You wanna tell us what's goin' on?' he veered hard left and then right into City Road, where he surprised everyone by pulling up next to the curb.

It was o-three hundred and still dark.

The other four men were all staring at him, but it was Bugs who piped up. 'Why are we stoppin' here?'

Ben's only answer was to lift his chin toward a black van parked under a streetlight thirty metres down the road. Bugs peered through the windscreen and then threw Ben a shrewd glance. Turning to Wolf he said, 'I think this one's for you, Wolfman.'

Frowning, Wolf leaned forward to squint down the road, then sucked in a breath and his eyes widened.

The woman leaning on the front of the black Ford Transit was staring back at the Humvee. When she straightened and waved, Wolf's hands fumbled with the door release in his rush to get out.

Heart pounding in his chest, he sprinted toward her, his legs finding renewed strength as he lengthened his stride.

She gazed at him in disbelief, and as he drew near she took an involuntary step forward, wonder and then elation playing over her face.

When he stopped a short distance in front of her she said softly, 'Do you remember me, Troy?'

In answer, he took the chain from around his neck and moved closer to place it over her head, saying gruffly, 'I remember everything.'

When she threw her arms around his neck he closed his eyes, overwhelmed by emotion, and pulled her tight against him. He said brokenly, 'Is your answer still yes?'

Drawing back to take hold of the ring, Modeen yanked it loose, uncaring when the chain slid to the road. Locking eyes with him, she threaded the ring onto the fourth finger of her left hand and threw her arms back around his neck. 'My answer is still yes.'

Four sets of eyes watched the tender scene from inside the Humvee. From their front seat positions, Ben and Bugs had the best view. Both were smiling.

Bugs gave a wolf whistle and then turned to the other two in the back seat with a goofy grin. 'Crikey,' he chirped, 'the wolfman doesn't muck around.'

'And why would he?' Salty grinned, 'he's got some lost time to make up.' His grin widened as he leaned forward to thump Bugs on a beefy shoulder. 'I love a happy ending, don't you?'

Ben started the Humvee and nosed it closer to the reunited couple, who appeared oblivious to all else but each other. When the four men jumped out and gathered around them, taking turns to slap Wolf heartily on the back, Modeen smiled her thanks and hugged each one of them.

When Bugs pulled back with a loud, 'Phew!' she frowned at him.

'What?'

'It's great to see you 'n all that, Modeen, but I have to say … you stink.'

'Thank you very much.' She raised an eyebrow and threw him a lop-sided grin. 'You know what it's like when you haven't showered for a week or more.' Leaving him wryly laughing, she pulled Ben aside and led him to the van. After opening the sliding door she stepped to one side, saying, 'I don't know who they are, but I believe one of them was ASIO and the other one was high up in the Mambas.'

Ben bent to stare at the corpses on the floor of the van and said stiffly, 'The agent was on surveillance ... I guess he got too close.' Straightening, he muttered, 'And the Mamba is Edward Moran.'

When Modeen murmured, 'Number one on my list,' Ben nodded. 'Yes, but number two in their organisation. Owen Patel is the leader. He has a tattooed mouth, blue eyes and dreadlocks.'

Modeen's lips tightened and she said flatly, 'Yes ... we met.'

'You can cross the second name off the list,' Spooky said, coming up behind them. 'Wiremu Kauri was the limo driver. I recognised him by the tattoo on what's left of his face.'

Modeen frowned. 'So where is Patel?' As she spoke, Wolf walked up to take her hand. Her expression softened when she looked up at him.

'Last time I saw him, he was in the back seat of the limo.' Ben turned to Wolf. 'Did you see anyone else in the Chrysler?'

'I was concentrating on the driver,' Wolf said, tearing

his eyes away from Modeen's smiling face for a second. 'But I'm pretty sure I could see two silhouettes in the vehicle when I took the shot.'

Ben shook his head. 'Well then … I guess Patel's still out there.'

# # #

If you've enjoyed MODEEN ROGUE I hope you'll consider posting a review on your retailer's site.
FHJ

FROM NATSEC FILES

Name: Josephine Dakota MODEEN

NatSec Alias: Josephine BENNET

Parents: John and Freda MODEEN

Siblings: Nil **Spouse:** Nil **Children:** Nil

DOB: 09/05/1986

Height: 5'11"

Hair: Platinum blonde, cropped short

Eyes: China blue

Character: Tough, clever, street-smart, courageous and decisive; has quick reflexes; can appear cool and aloof

Appearance: Tall, athletic, dresses boyishly but can be ultra-feminine when she chooses; has a strong but pretty face with fine features; normally wears a serious, self-possessed expression; has a scar on one cheek from a glancing bullet, and a deep scar on her left shoulder from a bullet that passed through the soft tissue

Private transport: Midnight blue Kawasaki GTR 1400cc motorbike

Weapon/s of choice: Walther PPX .9mm (referred to as "Walt")

Jobs: Soldier Regular Army; SASR specialist signaller and recipient of Medal of Gallantry and various service medals; Security Guard; NatSec Agent – Beta Team

Status: ROGUE

PRAISE FOR FRANK H JORDAN

'Holy Butt Kickers Batman! Frank Jordan can write a wicked story that mixes humor, adventure, and intrigue woven into a realistic plot. His characters are gritty and tough as nails. Love the accents and the people of Oz.'

— US REVIEWER

… [Jordan has] created a match for the baddies in Jo Modeen, a kick-ass heroine with nerves of steel and a size 9 boot….'

— THE CAIRNS POST NEWSPAPER

'There ain't nuthin' [sic] to dislike about Jo Modeen. Would love to [have] had her on our team back in Cambodia and Laos!'

— REVIEWER JR LEE

OTHER BOOKS IN THE SERIES

THE MODEEN TRANSFORMATION

The 2nd action-filled Modeen adventure

Australian security agencies are on alert in the lead-up to the 2014 international G20 Summit being held in Brisbane, Queensland. Although aware of an increase in web activity on the summit site and into the backgrounds of its attending diplomats, even NatSec intel can't know what the terrorist group known as 'The Spear of Allah' is planning.
Something ex-SASR soldier and now NatSec agent, Jo Modeen, is about to find out in a very personal way....

MODEEN: RULES OF ENGAGEMENT

The 7th thrilling instalment

Modeen and other members of her old squad find
themselves defending honour and truth, after being
subpoenaed to provide statements to a military inquiry
into allegations of war crimes.

Did Ben and his Special Forces squad blatantly breach
the ADF's Rules of Engagement while on deployment, or
is something more sinister afoot?

In *Modeen Convergence*, Modeen's team converges in far north Queensland on what becomes a complex mission with dangerous links to the past.

In *Modeen Rogue*, our heroine embarks on an unauthorised campaign of retribution. She's going rogue … and going alone.

In *Modeen Redemption*, NatSec is tasked with keeping safe the DOD's latest and most advanced weapon. A weapon that could alter the course of modern warfare. And must be kept secure at all costs….

The second box set is available as an ebook from your favourite online retailer.